Cintani Bird

2nd Edition

JIM CASH

ISBN: 1540426343
ISBN-13: 978-1540426345

DEDICATION

To my family and friends, who encouraged me
and allowed my mind to wander.

COVER DESIGN

Jen Street

www.thejenstreet.com

Editing by
Encouraging Word
Publishing Services
mceditor.com

TABLE OF CONTENTS

1 PROLOGUE

"Tell me old man, tell me what you know and you may live out your miserable life here in this shack of a house!

The big rough hand clamped around the aged throat and scarcely a whisper of air could enter or escape. The thin, gray haired man's boney fingers raked in vain at the thick fingers that cut off his air supply and his eyes grew wide.

"It was only a story for children! I know nothing of it!"

There was a long, low growl and the grip tightened even more.

"I will not linger much longer nor will you if you lie to me again! Where is it hidden and where are your kin?"

The old man was allowed to take a breath but his answer did not please his assailant. "You will never see it or my children! They have left this land to be sure and sailed beyond your reach!"

"You are mistaken old fool! One of your own has betrayed you and given us the keys to the door. I have only to find it and open the way! All you have guarded is lost. All you have hoped for is mine!"

The old man could no longer hear him for the wicked hand had crushed his windpipe and let him crumpled lifeless to the floor.

2 LUCCA AND SOPHIA

Sophia awoke slowly to the calls of sea birds and the morning sun streaming through her upstairs window. The shutters were open and the warm sea breeze was wafting through the room driving out the cold left behind by the night fog. Kicking away the thick quilt and soft sheets, her toes welcomed the freedom as she stretched out on top of the covers in a very long and satisfying yawn.

Through the window she watched the familiar sight of scant clouds and the sudden appearance and disappearance of the noisy gulls. They darted this way and that as they pursued their breakfast of unwilling fish and crustaceans.

Despite her unpleasant dreams, there was a smile on her face as she brushed her long brown hair and remembered her plans for the day. It was an outing Sophia had looked forward to and the morning sun was giving its blessing, warm and bright. The morning sun on the island of Yakolai was most always pleasant but Sophia deemed it even more so today.

With a hurried breakfast and a kiss to her mother's cheek, she bounced down the stairs to the street. Sophia's mother turned and followed her to the door and watched Sophia undo the lock and chain from her bicycle.

"I rather wish you were staying home tonight; It's not proper for a girl to be gone with a man so long!"

Sophia grinned as she fastened her basket to the bike.

"Oh Momma, you know it will be fine. We're going to be at his aunt's house and she's more old fashioned than you are!" There was a hurt look on Momma's face that prompted Sophia to return to her for another hug and a kiss on the cheek.

"Momma, you know that I love you, I didn't mean anything by that but this is 1950 and I'm a big girl now. I'm going to be fine! Besides, Lucca you've known since a baby!"

Momma's arms remained crossed as Sophia tried to convince her to not worry but she held on to her pout just a little longer. "He's no baby any more; see that he minds his manners!"

Seeing that she had blessing in spite of objection, Sophia kissed her again and picked up her bicycle. "I love you Momma, I'll see you tomorrow!"

Lucca had invited her down the coast to his Aunt and Uncle's home and also promised her a picnic on this day, though he would not tell her much more. He had only said to be ready early and to meet him by the old bridge on the north road. With sweater tied round her waist, she pushed off from the sidewalk and pedaled up the bumpy cobblestone toward the center of town.

She passed the old women with heads together trading gossip as they pretended to sweep the walk. Old men smoking their first pipe of the day looked at the sky, to predict how warm it would be, even though the temperature rarely varied more than two or three degrees this time of the year.

Sophia waved and both men and women returned the greeting with a confused countenance. They had no real objection to her being there; it was just that a beautiful girl cycling by at this time of the morning was not something they were used to seeing. Very few things ever changed here in the village of Kerdaino and for most of the people that was the way they liked it. Two world wars had even come and gone and completely passed the little island by. There was just so little reason for the outside world to notice this tiny dot in the sea.

The center of town was still asleep when she passed the fountain and headed out toward the bridge. When she reached it, Lucca was leaning against the ivy covered stone column at the far end. He waived to her as she crossed the midway point of the old stone arch and walked out to meet her.

"Good morning! Are you ready?"

Sophia coasted to a stop in front of him and smiled that mischievous smile that he loved so much.

"I am, but I must say that my mother was a little concerned about me riding off alone with a strange man this morning!"

Lucca gave a poor attempt at being insulted, crossing his arms and sticking out his lower lip. "She was there when my mother gave birth and she calls me a stranger?"

Sophia laughed, "Well, you were gone for a long time,

and since you've returned she hasn't seen much of you!"

He continued his feeble attempt to be hurt,

"She didn't forget you when you were away at school did she?

"Well, not entirely, because I wrote her letters every week! I'm sure if you had done that, she would be more understanding."

The pout quickly left his face and he threw a leg over his bicycle.

"Then I will have to come introduce myself to her and maybe she will remember me!"

With another laugh, they set out on the road that followed the coastline cliffs of the west and away from the rich farmland soil in the south highlands. They passed donkey carts stacked high with hay and peddlers heading for market the way they had for hundreds of years. It could have just been her light heart that day or maybe the weather brought it about, but everyone they met seemed to be happy and waved warmly. Either way, she would not question or debate it, only embrace it fully.

After the long ride along the winding cliff road, they took a path where the trees grew thick and the trail was little traveled. It was quite bumpy because of the large round stones exposed by the winter rains and the thick branches overhead kept most of the sunlight out. Sophia was glad in this cool dark place that she had remembered her sweater.

She slowed to a stop and Lucca looked back just as her feet touched the ground and reached for the woolen garment around her waist. The air was moist amidst the tall ferns and Sophia took in the musty smell of thick moss. Lucca stopped as well and the quiet stillness of this place enveloped the both of them with a sense of wonderment and delight.

With almost reverence, Sophia's eyes absorbed the hue of rich browns and the countless shades of green on every side. She felt sound in the colors that called to something within her and for a moment, washed away every care.

Lucca loved this place too and didn't mind the delay in the least. The image of Sophia's smile in that moment, in that place would return to him many times. With it would come a wisp of sweetness; like a drop of honey on the tip of his tongue. Sophia would also recall how closely they seemed to share those feelings though they were some distance apart on the trail. Not until the distant voice of a raven drifted through did either stir and when Sophia reluctantly put foot to pedal, Lucca silently turned to push off as well.

It was more than a mile before sunlight flooded the trail again and Sophia caught up with Lucca who was already dismounted. When her eyes adjusted to the bright day again she saw the old stone tower high above them. Its foundation sat just above the tops of the trees on a dry shale covered hill and the path to the small plateau in front of it zigzagged several times. It was obviously too steep and narrow to ride.

"You will be in serious trouble if I tell my mother that you brought me here! I know that your parents don't approve of this place either. Aren't you afraid of the ghosts we heard about in school?"

Lucca took her teasing in stride, grinning sheepishly as he tucked the bicycles behind a dull green clump of brush. With his backpack in place he stood at attention and saluted her solemnly.

"I promise that I will fight to the death any ghosts that we see!" Certainly, she did not believe the stories children told, but it was true that no one she knew ever came up here. She always thought it odd that her parents never spoke of this place either. As she followed Lucca up the high hill to the base of the tower she remembered how her grandfather would warn her that the ground here was soft, like quicksand and would swallow you up in its depths. So never wanting to be swallowed up, she decided as a child to stay away.

At the corner of the third and last switchback, Sophia paused and looked back over the tops of the trees at the ocean beyond. She thought this must be what the ravens see as they sway on the highest perch of the evergreens. She envied the view but was thankful that the ground was not moving.

There was no good reason why she had not come here as she grew older other than it had not occurred to her to do so. Life was full of schooling and travel and she had all but forgotten this place. But now as she stood with the tower above her and the deep blue of the sea stretching out endlessly before her, the adventure took hold of her sensibility and threw it to the gusting ocean breezes.

She decided that a picnic in a forbidden tower with a handsome rebel was just what she needed. In this slow moving island world it was far too easy to settle into the footsteps of past generations. They were worn deep into the path of history and it took conscious effort to step outside of them.

With another moment's rest at the top of the trail, they continued upward. Lucca led as their feet left the earth and climbed the steep, broken steps to the top of the tower. There was little but broken ruins on dry ground ambling up the mountain behind them, but the view from the top turret in all other directions was something to see. They could see all the way to Totolli in the north then, down beyond the village to the cliffs of Imanado some thirty miles in the south.

Totolli was northern most tip of the island where the waters are shallow and exposed to the open sea winds making it unsuitable for boats and living. There are a few abandoned shacks there but no people. The high rock walls of Imanado are the first thing that mainlanders would see as they arrive on the ferry from the south but they would not see the rich soiled crop land that stretches out above them. From this angle, Sophia could see how the cliffs jutted up and outward over the sea resembling the proud bow of a huge ship. This angle and shape protects the fields and trees above it from most all of the hard winter winds and holds the good earth up to the bright summer sun. Even the small island of Votadi was now visible far, far out in the blue of the sea in front of them as they sat down to share a meal of fresh bread, several wonderful cheeses and a favorite wine.

The two discussed the past month's events in great detail as both had been off the island and had only a short time ago returned. Lucca listened and laughed as Sophia brought him up to date on all the latest village happenings and gossip. She giggled at his stories from his fishing crew's antics at sea, wondering how much of it was really true though he swore it was.

Without either one noticing, the morning hours evaporated amidst their laughter and the sun was high above them. As its rays warmed Sophia's olive skin she closed her eyes and leaned back against the cool stone wall. She soaked in the sound of the wind singing soft ballads of long ago as it whipped in and through the cracks of the tower. Lucca sat quietly also but his eyes were open and his gaze was fixed upon the lovely young woman that dreamed some secret dream.

Could it be of fearful dragons and tall towers like this

one, of looking a far off for signs of a rescuer? Might she be watching as the brave knight dashes headlong into danger against a horrible foe, risking all for the lady in peril? And could she he wondered, just perhaps, when the beast is slain, be seeing his face appear as the helmet is removed. The daydream carried him away for some time and the fair maiden dozed blissfully.

It was the typical story when they were young. He was the one that teased the little girl down the road and threw rocks at her goats. She was the one who pretended to ignore him some years later when she had become a lovely young girl going to the market place to shop for her mother.

Later, it seemed that the tables reversed again as he began making his way in the world. She watched from a distance as this handsome young man loaded nets onto his family's fishing boat and it seemed it went on this way for years. It was like the timing of their lives had slipped a cog and kept them forever just inches away from ever connecting. Then suddenly, on that first evening of the summer festival they both turned around and were face to face, seeing each other in a way that neither one expected.

The chance meeting caught both off guard and perhaps this festive atmosphere persuaded each of them to leave defenses down just long enough to realize how much they had in common. Growing up just yards apart, they took for granted how their heritage had woven itself together. The triumphs and tragedies of the village had made an imprint on both of them and it looked much the same no matter which one was examined.

That was probably why it felt so natural to just walk and talk as they finally relaxed and just spoke plainly with one another. Each realized that they now enjoyed the company and there was no longer any need to defend or attack.

Now, the only real tension between them was that created by the growing possibility of a romance. Neither spoke of it but almost instantly both were aware of it. It was a giddy anticipation that grew from that night to this day and intensified by the deliberate act of ignoring it.

Sophia stirred and opened her eyes to see the young man of her dreaming still present and she smiled at him as she tucked her secret thoughts back away. But Lucca sliced off more bread and began to tell her secrets of his own.

"There are a lot of stories about this place, most of them are made up by people like our parents to keep us away from here but I know the real one."

Sophia sat up to listen to another of his wild tales and was sure she would enjoy this one. Sophia had always loved hearing the old stories for some reason and true or not, she loved imagining herself in them in some way.

"So you know the truth about this city?"

"That's right, are you interested?"

"Oh by all means yes, I am! Please, tell me!"

Lucca leaned in toward her and whispered,

"Few know the real name of this place and I only tell you now because the wind will keep it secret between you and me!"

Sophia could not resist a giggle as she too leaned toward Lucca and enjoyed the closeness of their lips. Lucca was to her disappointment, only trying to keep his voice down and he looked from side to side before he spoke.

"Since the time of Christ, this was Menuchah, the city of quiet waters and the Cintanians!"

Sophia's blank stare told Lucca that she was unmoved by his great revelation so for the next hour, he spoke in hushed tones of how by chance, a Roman army had landed there nearly two thousand years ago and decided to stay.

Soon Sophia was truly excited by his tale of the villagers who fought hard even though they were outnumbered by the ship loads of battle hardened soldiers.

Word from Caesar commanded that any building that spoke of their culture be destroyed. All flags were torn down, all paintings and books were burned and the homes of all leaders were demolished. Only the old tower was left as a warning visible by land or sea, that none should dare stand against Rome. Those who would not bow to the great empire hid by day then struck out at the garrisons by night. Lucca's voice rose and fell with each battle he described and Sophia found him most believable.

"When the soldiers gave chase," Lucca explained, "their attackers would dart back through hidden doorways to the underground. Finally, Rome ordered a massacre of every man, woman and child that would not bow to the Caesar as God and that was when it happened."

"What happened?" Sophia said.

"Before the order could be carried out, every bit of the resistance disappeared and was never seen again!"

Sophia sat wide-eyed waiting for more but Lucca paused.

"Where did they go?"

Another long moment past then he smiled and casually asked,

"More cheese?"

The shift interrupted her imagining and she punched him in the arm. Lucca let out a half-hearted yelp but then laughed as he took a bite of bread.

With the sun now past the midday point and leaning into the western sky, it cast a slight shadow from the tower across the edge of the crumbling walls below. Sophia gazed out at the stones imagining all before their destruction. She saw the narrow streets filled with people streaming in and out of the city gates like so many insects.

All were driven to complete their tasks of buying, selling, bartering and trading and their voices rose daily to the ears of the watchman that would sit in this tower.

It was a sound that Sophia had heard before as she had sat beside the brook at Copani and the waters splashed down through the smooth stones on their way to the sea. Each droplet excited to take the journey toward its destiny had absolutely no control over its path, yet all moved together with the same goal.

She remembered a silly sadness as she watched some drops splashing out on the bank as others were permitted to continue on. Then she realized that if it were not for those droplets seemingly sacrificed along the way, she would not be sitting among the cool green grass and smelling the sweet perfume of the flowers that also sprang up around her there.

So it was she thought; that this city had fallen into dry ruin because the people had ceased to flow through and bring life as they rushed on to their many destinations. Now, only a few rarely used paths remained. They were probably traveled mostly by the jackal and frightened rabbits. Not even the scrubby Taba trees grew up through the powdery stone fragments and it saddened her to see such an absence of life.

Lucca packed the rest of their bread and cheese into his backpack.

"I want to show you something; are you ready to explore a little"?

Sophia roused from her daydreaming and turned toward the young man that now stood over her extending his hand.

"Is that all of the story?"

"Oh no, there's much more, come on."

Lucca was not tall but he was handsome as far as Sophia was concerned. He worked hard on his boat and it showed in his strong arms and lean torso. It was no effort at all for him to pull her to her feet and her heart felt funny as they looked into each other's eyes for that brief moment before he turned away. Her hand however, was still in his as he led her down the stairs.

Sophia knew she was fully capable of descending on her own and at an earlier time in their lives would have been hugely insulted and protested loudly. But today she was rather enjoying the feel of his strong hand gently wrapped around hers and she sensed that he too was not just interested in her safety. At the foot of the steps and out onto the eastern path, they remained hand in hand.

3 PA-MA-TO-LEA

Lucca rambled on about this building and that as his deep blue eyes searched the rubble ahead but now and then he would scan the trail behind them. It was as though he half expected to see someone there but there was only an occasional swirl of dust as the east and west winds met and squabbled briefly over the dry earth.

Sophia listened for a while but eventually the words fell in her mind like the white noise of soft rain on the rooftop. The feel of Lucca's hand around hers had whisked Sophia far away to another path where the ground was not dry and barren like this place. It was a place where green fields were filled with small white flowers. She still walked hand in hand with someone, but the low sun was so much in her eyes that she could only see a form. Then, little by little the sun moved and the person she skipped along with in the picture came into focus. It was her father and she was a little girl again as they walked to town.

He was tall and strong and she felt safe and happy. She had not felt this way for a very long time, perhaps because of his death several years ago. She found herself wanting this peacefulness to go on and on but in time the memory merged with the present on the edge of the dry white trail.

There in the dust was a clump of those same small white flowers defying the arid hillside and thriving among the rocks. They were so close to the color of the stone she had not seen them from the tower and yet now she could see them dotting every hillside around her.

"Those are called "Pa-mo-to-lea," Lucca said. "They are said to grow on the place where each Cintanian soldier fell and bled. The name means, "'Cry for justice'" in the old tongue."

Sophia stooped and cradled a bunch with her hand and marveled at how something so delicate could survive this place. Sophia's face scrunched up with a question.

"Old tongue? What old tongue?"

"The petals," Lucca continued, "are shaped like the tears of their lovers that returned to weep each day over the ground where they died. When the Romans finally drove them away, the flowers remained to keep watch forever."

Before Lucca led on, Sophia rose and placed one in her hair. The living legends enticed her to hear more stories about this secret people that existed so close to her home without her even knowing. She had no idea that Lucca's imagination was so vivid.

"Why were they so mean to them," she asked?

Lucca looked at the flower and seemed to lose

concentration for a moment but quickly recovered.

"It was forbidden by Rome to even speak their own language or of any god but Caesar. The people were punished if a single word of it was heard by the soldiers. They wanted them to become and speak as the Romans and forget their old ways."

"But they wouldn't, would they?"

Lucca shook his head as he peeked over the short stone wall of a well and jumped up on the edge. He held onto the decaying cross beam and held his hand out to Sophia.

She grasped his hand was pulled to the top of the wall, but there was not a filled in well as she had expected but a dark open shaft. Just below ground level, the rusty rungs of an iron ladder disappeared into the darkness.

"This is where the real story begins. Be careful to hold on tight!"

Lucca stepped down onto the ladder and looked back up at her, his voice slightly mysterious.

"After the disappearance of the Cintanians on the island, the remaining outsiders were very compliant and Rome saw no need for a garrison to stay. When they pulled out, they warned the people not to seek freedom from tribute to Rome and spies were left among them to keep the people in fear. If a man even spoke against Caesar, it wasn't long before he was found dead in the city plaza."

Sophia watched the stone flake away around the ladder's support system as Lucca put his full weight on it and started to reconsider following.

"The island repopulated mildly and the rebellion was erased from the history books in hope of attracting trade ships. Most of the secret assassins they called "Tarantadei" were eventually themselves killed by the villagers when hard drinking would bring one to bragging and his purposes would be discovered. When sleep overtook him, the men would discreetly come and smother him. The hunters were themselves being hunted."

Sophia wrinkled her nose and pushed that thought aside.

"So they got rid of them, right?"

Lucca's voice hid something as he stopped to look back up at her and reply.

"Not all were found and some were known to escape to the mainland. Notes were found in houses with vows to return and have vengeance and no one was certain that others were not still hiding in the mountains to the south. Now and then a defiant politician would mysteriously fall to his death or just disappear and most were sure that it was not by accident."

Sophia nervously mounted the ladder above Lucca and slowly the pair descended into the cool air below. It was not a frighteningly deep hole but at the bottom of the well were stone steps that descended quickly into the darkness of the earth. Lucca took her hand again and in a moment's time Sophia could not see either in front of her.

At the end of the steps her feet found flat ground and Lucca struck a match to a lantern no doubt left there on a previous visit. Light now drenched the walls and there was as Sophia had expected, a passage leading eastward under the city.

Sophia's wide eyes told Lucca she was impressed and he smiled that smile and stepped forward.

Watch your head!"

The walls here were not the same crumbling white stone as on the surface but solid. The bubbly texture reminded her of the dark colored candy she had helped her mother make after they had heated sweet syrup to a boil and poured it out on a board to harden. Lucca guessed her question as she lightly rubbed a finger over the stone.

"When the volcano rose from the sea to make our island, lava flowed down the slopes to the sea. The outer shell cooled quickly but the hot center flowed on, leaving hundreds of tunnels under the surface. They would have been easy to find then because you could see the lava stream on top of the ground, but more eruptions sent up tons of white ash that buried them all."

Sophia imagined just how it might have looked as probably for weeks or even months the earth rumbled and molten magma rolled out of its belly across the newly formed landmass. When the fiery anger began to subside, the ominous hissing and spewing of dust into the atmosphere remained for untold time. Up, up, up went the smoke and ash until she thought God himself turned it away from the Heavens and back toward the land it was birthed from. Like a deadly smothering snow, it covered the land, filling in every low place and making the mountains smooth.

"No one knows who found them first," Lucca supposed, "sometime before Rome came I'm sure. The Cintanians linked them together and somehow kept them secret even from Caesar. That's how leaders of the cause survived."

The rounded ceiling rose and fell from time to time as Sophia followed Lucca through the cool air but the lantern gave off plenty of light to see the changing height. The floor seemed to be sloping slightly up hill but as the air grew colder, Sophia still sensed that they were moving deeper under the earth. Lucca seemed at ease as he led past dark side tunnels without even giving them a glance. From time to time he pointed out strange markings on the wall and told her how he was using them to navigate.

"You see, in each circle there is a bird,"

"Yes, I see it!"

A distance down the way he stopped at another one on her left and pointed to the center. "Do you see that this one has one less feather on his wing and is now flying a different direction?"

Sophia stared at the small drawing and then turned to her right. There was the side passage the tiny bird was pointing to.

"Is that our path?" she asked excitedly.

Lucca Smiled at the sparkle in her dark eyes and nodded. She followed him through the somewhat smaller opening that required them to walk in a crouching position for some fifty yards or more until it reached a parallel tunnel where they could stand upright again. This time she spotted the small, almost hidden symbol on her own with its flight headed back to the east.

Not too far ahead there were many markings on the walls. In fact, the drawings became very detailed and linked together in a streaming mural. It was hard to walk and take in everything but Sophia began to see a story unfolding in the forms painted beside her. Lucca allowed her to move along slowly and she watched history play out in the light of the lantern.

"Is that the tower Lucca?"

He nodded and she touched the picture of a spire against a cloudy sky. Lucca returned to her and examined the painting with her.

"Then this must be how the city once looked! You didn't make this up!"

Behind the tower she saw ornate buildings and a beautiful fountain just inside the city gates. She saw that their path to the well had taken them straight through the heart of the city as it must have stood so long ago.

Further on the scene began to darken as soldiers appeared in the streets, pulling down statues and pointing spears at women and children. A little further down a man stood hands bound behind him as a soldier raised his sword overhead. The faces in the crowd were full of sorrow and it was plain that this was a man greatly admired.

Now images of battles were common and nameless heroes were depicted leading raids against overwhelming forces then escaping them by vanishing into the caves. She thought it curious that tributes were made in picture to Cintanian and Roman military men alike. It seemed that some Romans were sympathetic to the oppressed people and would secretly show mercy to them. But over all, the stories pierced Sophia's heart with their sadness and fear.

"Here we are."

Sophia turned to Lucca, "What is this?"

She had been so enamored by the paintings that she hadn't realized that Lucca had stopped in front of a thick, wooden door on the opposite wall. It was the first real door they had seen but it was not finely carved or inlaid with precious metal; it was just a thick, well made door that swung open at the weight of Lucca's palm against it.

To Sophia's astonishment, Lucca turned off the lantern revealing the presence of light already inside. In the corner of the room a small table held a large glass bowl filled with water. Above it, through the cciling, a beam of light shot smooth edged down to its center where it fragmented and illuminated the entire room. But the glass was very old and the discoloration painted every wall with rainbow hues that seemed to change and move wherever she walked.

She had no words for a long time as she took in the sight of dozens of old books filling shelves along the back wall. Lucca also stood gazing somberly at the rows of books in an almost reverent manner.

"How do you know of this place? Why don't I know about these stories?"

Lucca turned to her but paused a moment as though retrieving the memory.

"I was a little boy when I heard my grandfather come in speaking the old tongue. Grandmother became very angry and told him to be quiet and stay away from that place but I thought she meant the tavern. The next day I asked him what place she meant and to teach me the funny words. He scolded me and would not speak of it again so of course, that only made me more curious! I remember how exciting it was when I climbed out of bed and followed him one summer evening from my uncle's house to the well. When he disappeared, I gathered up my courage to climb down here with my own little flashlight."

"And you found this all on your own?"

"No, I got lost and wandered around thinking I would die down here."

Sophia's giggle escaped before she could control it and she quickly reached out to Lucca and took his hands, trying to stop.

"I'm sorry; I couldn't help it, I just…"

Seconds later, both of them were laughing and the tension that had enthralled her with his tale up to this point vanished with his unexpected answer. Their hands remained linked as he continued his story and her eyes remained fixed on his.

"I sat crying until I finally fell asleep and woke up with a hand on my shoulder and Grandfather's voice in my ear. He had heard my sobbing echoing through the tunnels and finally searched me out. I thought he would beat me but instead he brought me here and quietly began telling me of our past."

"Of your past; your family is Cintanian?'

Lucca nodded,

"He taught me the old tongue but only after I swore never to speak it anywhere but here and least of all around my grandmother! We read most all of these books together and often he would have me read to him from what he called a very special book. There were beautiful drawings like the other books but there was always something more that stirred in me when he let me read from it. He said it was more important than all the others and he kept it hidden; even from me. He made me vow never to bring anyone here or speak of it unless it was a matter of life and death."

Sophia's smile changed and the question that filled her mind was clearly visible on her face.

"Yet," she spoke softly, "Here we are."

Lucca's smile had faded also and his eyes left hers to the floor. It was an awkward moment of silence before he spoke again.

"Since my grandfather died, to this day I have kept my promise and I have not broken it now. There are things I must tell you, Sophia."

Lucca began to explain to Sophia how he had been taught to read these histories and the special book since he was a boy. He had left the island in his late teens to find work and adventure and seldom thought of this place until the news of his grandfather's death came to him. When he eventually returned, bought the fishing boat and hired a crew, the worries of money and responsibility afforded him even less time.

Then, bad fishing weather came and life slowed. That was when he felt the pull to return and read again. He reread the tales about one special book and how it contained verses said to bring good crops when prayed to Elyan, the Cintani god. Other phrases when said out loud would bring victory in battle. The reader of this one book could even heal wounds and see the motives of a man's heart.

All Cintanians pledged to protect this book at any cost. It was the center of their culture and could not be lost. Every child was taught some part to hold on to and in the dark days, they would gather and recite the portion they had learned. The writers spoke of courage and hope that rose in their hearts until it could be felt in the room and the old mountain rumbled. He had never felt this room shake but he remembered that stir within him.

"It was then I understood it to be the book my grandfather kept hidden from me but stories said different. The book was supposed to have gone with the Cintanians when they disappeared yet everything I read sounded like Grandfather's book. I looked for clues and searched every tunnel for it. Something in my heart said it was still hidden here."

Sophia was fascinated but still very confused so she ventured the question again. "But who is in danger? Why is this life and death?"

Lucca stared at the wall, obviously reluctant to continue but knowing he must.

"Remember I told you about the Tarantadei that were never found?

Sophia nodded, "The assassins, yes."

"They too took an oath by their gods, to not only seek out and kill all Cintanians but also to steal the book and bring it to Caesar. The Tarantadei were part of a dark eastern cult called Darjan that Caesar himself probably feared. His decree to let them remain in Rome was never understood by even those in his own council because the Darjan were never required as all others to pay tribute. Some writings even suggested that failure to compensate Darjan fairly for the use of the Tarantadei was directly linked to Caesar's death. In any case, it was an evil partnering to be sure.

They vowed that if they failed, they would raise their children up in hatred of this race and have them swear to carry on the mission. No descendant of theirs would rest until the book was captured and this people totally wiped out. The Tarantadei were so loyal to their gods that even when Rome had forgotten them and this tiny island; they still vowed to cleanse the land of the resisting Cintanians. Even hundred of years after Rome fell, few dare to keep the old tongue alive and now only in whispers!"

Sophia let go a little nervous laugh and moved in front of him to see his eyes again.

"That was nearly two *thousand* year ago Lucca. You don't believe that those people are trying to kill you now do you? Your grandfather's imagination really does have you believing in ghosts!"

She pulled on his sleeve playfully but the irritated scowl on his face made her realized how serious he was. Lucca stared at her for a moment and then swallowed hard before going on. He moved to the wall and withdrew a book. Opening it to a page he had marked, Lucca pointed to a crude picture of a venomous snake.

"I was in a tavern while off the island and I saw a man with a tattoo that sent chills through me. It was a symbol I had seen in this very book. The Cintanians found this mark branded on the bodies of every assassin they killed. When I saw it on this man's neck, I moved close enough to hear him questioning the bar keep as to the whereabouts of a local man. He learned the address, slipped the barkeep a large fist of money and quickly left the pub. I tried to follow him but he disappeared too quickly and I got lost in the evening fog and went back to the tavern.

The next day I too asked for directions and found the house the man was looking for. But I was not going to be able to speak to him. The old man had been killed that night; strangled while his wife slept in the next room. The poor woman was wailing and sobbing as the police carried away his limp body. I thought at first I was imagining what she was saying so I went closer. It made no sense to anyone else but I knew the one word she cried over and over."

Lucca's eyes turned to Sophia and looked at the flower in her hair.

"Pa-mo-to-lea."

Sophia's hand slowly reached up to touch the white petals and for the first time she was truly frightened in this place for this was not the Lucca she came here with.

"Why are you telling me all this Lucca? Are you trying to scare me?"

Suddenly his stern expression melted away and he took her hand again gently with both of his.

"No Sophia! No, I would never make you part of this! I only wish I could keep it from you but I think you deserve to know!"

He could see the anger and confusion in her eyes as she pulled away from him.

"What do you mean? You're not making sense. Why

does this concern me?"

Lucca filled his lungs with air as if to shout at her. She cringed and braced for it but he held back, letting out only a long weary sigh as his body deflated on to the wooden bench. Sophia saw his tearful eyes and returned to put her arm around his sagging shoulders.

"Tell me Lucca, tell me." Her anger was also gone and the softness of her voice bid him continue.

Lucca checked her eyes for sincerity before he stood again and walked to the old oak door. He stretched to the top edge of the header and removed a thin panel over a hollowed out space hidden there. A thick, leather bound volume not much larger than his hand was withdrawn and returned to the table where Sophia stood.

"It was hidden so simply and yet I had past it by a hundred times. It would still be lost if I hadn't been up on the bench oiling the old hinges. Grandfather said that I would find it when it was in need of being found and only an heir of the book of ages would know where to look."

His palms were sweaty and Sophia saw trepidation in his eyes as he slowly lifted the cover and showed her the first page.

"This is a list of the five lineages that survive here on the Island and both our family lines are here in the pages. I also traced the man that was killed back through to a sixth that left here some hundred years ago. It rattled me so much that I closed the book and haven't had it open since."

Lucca searched her eyes now for some sign that she believed him as he took another breath.

"I put it away but came back later to look for anything that might help me find the old man's murderer. That's when I found a man's footprints that were not mine on the floor. Someone else knows of this place and I'm afraid that in time they will know how to find the families too."

With a weak smile Lucca locked eyes with Sophia and finished his tale, "I need your help to convince our families that this crazy story is real!"

Sophia felt the strength ebbing out of her own legs now and slowly sat down on the bench herself. All was quiet for a moment then she spoke.

"I remember now, when I was very young, my grandmother would talk about seeing the Cintani tears but I never knew what she meant. She talked about the old language that her mother knew but never spoke to any one but her father, and then only whisperings. I thought it was just a game they had made up between them."

Lucca put his arm around her and she leaned into him.

"Whoever this is doesn't know the old tongue because he didn't look in any order or replace the books right. I think he was looking for symbols or drawings that would lead him to us. He will stay hidden, listening for the smallest word that would identify a descendant. If we can quietly warn everyone, we can all watch for an unfamiliar person and be careful of our words."

For the next few hours, Lucca opened the book explaining symbols and phrases to Sophia. There were many words that she had heard in her own home. She saw how easy it would be to discover Cintanian heritage in her village just by listening. It might be a single word spoken by her mother or an innocent phrase that contained a fragment of an ancient proverb. That night Sophia learned the names of the five families with Cintani blood that might be in danger.

It all depended on how much this intruder had

gleaned from these books himself. Lucca was not even sure if a real Tarantadei even existed. It might be just another member of the families that already knew of this place. If it was or wasn't, it was time that everyone talked anyway. Then there was the matter of when or where a possible killer might strike. Tradition held that they killed only at the peek of the harvest moon, yet the old man had died midway between.

"I hope this is all for nothing Sophia, but I would never forgive myself if I kept quiet and someone we love was hurt."

In a pause, Lucca stretched and gathered his thoughts while looking at the glass bowl in the corner.

"It's getting late; we should go."

Sophia rubbed her eyes and put the book down onto the table. It had been a much different day than she had expected and in many ways, she wished they had never come here. On the other hand, Lucca was right about one thing. She would not have believed any of this had she not seen it. There was something happening that would no doubt change her life forever. She felt the pulsing of destiny racing in this moment like fast moving blood through her veins.

Lucca rubbed the smooth leather of the one book's cover,

"I thought before that it would be safer here but we should take it with us now. It's the only book that holds the family names that must not be found out."

He wrapped the cloth that their bread had been in around the book and tucked it inside his pack.

"He doesn't know how to find us yet but it would only be a matter of time if he had this."

4 VOICES

They were threading back through the tunnels without much conversation at all and it proved to be a very good thing for when they got back to the place where they had to cross to the other tunnel they heard voices.

Lucca put his finger to his lips as he tried to zero in on just how close they were. His eyes darted back up the corridor, then back toward the direction where the words were becoming clearer. In a moment, he had made his decision and was pulling Sophia back the way they had come.

Just short of the book room he veered off into another passage. Sophia looked for a marking on the wall but saw none there. The way narrowed to no more than two feet across now but instead of slowing down, Lucca's pace quickened. To make matters worse, Sophia watched him turn the knob of the lantern and the light quickly faded away to only a faintly glowing strand within the glass. After handing it to her she felt him press her hand around the strap of his knapsack and she held on tight.

Feeling his way along the walls with both hands now, Lucca was half dragging her up a rough cut stairway. They reached the top in complete darkness and made a series of three left turns into other tunnels. Sophia was lost and breathing hard when a brilliant streak of light appeared over Lucca's shoulder and blinded her. They had stopped and soon her eyes adjusted to see the room around her.

She realized that the familiar beam was not only streaming down through the ceiling, but continued through the floor to the book room directly below. Lucca dropped to the floor beside the light and both worked to control the sound of their breathing as they listened for the voices again. Sophia crouched beside him and hoped they would never hear them, but soon the hinges of old oak door sounded and voices floated upward into her ears.

"So it is true, the Cintani hide like mice in the mountain."

The voice had a low, gravel filled tone of someone who had smoked for many years. The second voice was higher pitched and seemed to be nervously seeking approval like the apprentice of a hard master.

"It took me long to find the ruined city only because the old drunkard's mumbling made little sense. He would often fall asleep having told only the same old tale of a book of ages, night after night. Once he spoke of the Tower City, It was just a matter of following footprints to the well."

Pogis was a small time criminal in the mainland city of Sotro and was more of an annoyance to local police than anything else. They even at times looked the other way from his pilfering and swindles because he many times could be pressured into squealing on bigger fish swimming in his pond of corruption. He had spent a fair amount of time in the jails there but for the most part was not worth tracking down.

When the big man first approached him, Pogis feared that it was someone he had betrayed to the police, come for revenge. But the fear in his eyes turned to greedy delight when Balin thrust a fistful of gold coin into his and offered him even more if he would get the information he desired.

It was the sort of thing that Pogis was good at but a look at his new employer also told him that he should be careful not to fail. Balin was not a young man but his fists were calloused and his build was solid like that of a seasoned soldier. One look in his eyes and Pogis knew that this man was not to be crossed. Even now after delivering on his part of their agreement, he could not be at ease as Balin searched the room, muttering and growling.

"If he had only given us a surname or a crest, we would be sure to find these traitors! I find only their drivel and lies about bravery and nothing about who remains of this race of cowards! Here, take this one. There are symbols that I have seen before. "

As Lucca and Sophia sat in the darkness, they could hear them rifling through the bookshelves and hurriedly fluttering through the pages. Within a moment or two there would be a thud on the stone floor as the volume was tossed carelessly aside. Now and then Balin would choose one and throw it at Pogis who would stuff it in a sack.

"If you had not killed him so quickly," the little man offered, "perhaps he might have been persuaded to tell us more."

There was a sudden crashing sound, they guessed to be the old table being violently overturned as the Balin's voice exploded into the room.

"You know nothing! These are a stubborn and stupid race, like the oxen that graze without wit. I have seen his kind many times before! His foolish sense of honor would keep him straining against persuasion like a brainless mule resists even under the whip! No, I have grown weary of these, these sheep that chew and chew upon our land without right. They must be wiped out before they steal and eat every blade of grass on the fathers' land that they pollute!"

Through the hole, Lucca tried desperately to see the faces but could only catch glimpses of clothing and boots. It was this effort to discover that led to them being discovered, for as he peered into the opening, his head broke the beam of light that lit the lower room. When all had suddenly gone quiet after such a tumult, he realized what he had done and Sophia saw the anguish in his face

There was nothing left to do now but take flight and as Lucca took Sophia's hands and pulled her to her feet, she could hear the shouting and tramping of feet below them. She heard the big oak door fly open and smack against the rock wall. The assassin cursed and commanded his underling to find a way to the upper chamber but Lucca calmed himself and turned to Sophia.

"They will not find the way here for sometime but they will find it. I know another room that will keep us safe for now but I have to get close enough see their faces."

"That old one is crazy Lucca! We should stay hidden and wait for them to leave. We can be very quiet and they will think we have left."

Lucca shook his head. "They tracked me this far and I was always careful not to tread heavy. They will know that we have not climbed the well ladder or worse, will be waiting there when we do."

They moved through the darkness and not far from

the upper room Lucca pulled Sophia through another opening and pressed her into a tight low ceiling area. From there she guessed he would be able to ambush anyone that came by. They listened for the longest time to the echoing footsteps behind them and sat motionless in the darkness until Sophia could stand it no longer.

"How will we get past them," she whispered? She was afraid that even now they were close by.

Lucca gently squeezed her hand and tried to reassure her but he himself was uncertain of his own plan.

"There is another way out but I'm going to be sure they can't follow us first. Don't move, I'll be right back. Don't leave this spot, no matter what happens; do you promise?"

Sophia was shaking as she answered, 'Yes."

A second later his hand slipped from hers and he silently brushed past, out of the pocket and back down the corridors of stone.

It seemed ages that she huddled there listening to the distant crunching of boot against grit and stone. Now and then there would be a growling curse muttered as the Tarantadei would slip and fall on loose sand or reach a dead end and have to back track to the larger route again.

Each time she heard sound it seemed to be closer and the voice angrier. She felt like the small quail she had seen on walks with her father. When the dog caught its scent, it would not budge from its cover for the longest time. Sophia wished now that like the bird, she could rocket skyward and away on wildly beating wings but she held fast waiting for Lucca. She listened for his footsteps but instead, heard a low hissing begin like air from her bicycle tire.

The sound of hissing also echoed to the ears of Balin

and his guide when Lucca lit the fuse and ducked down. Their shouting and cursing began almost immediately as the two fell and tumbled back toward the main tunnel in hopes of reaching the well before being buried alive. They had no idea where the charge had been laid but were quite sure they were closer to it than they wanted to be.

The big man and his hireling had almost made the main tunnel when the dynamite ignited and the percussion that followed them knocked them to the ground. A cloud of dust and dirt filled the air and small fragments rained down from the cracking ceiling as Pogis grabbed at his ears in pain, expecting them to be bleeding. Balin was coughing and wiping his eyes after pulling himself up and searching blindly in the dust for the stairs to the ladder. He found them and when his hand struck metal he climbed the ladder toward the surface with no concern for Pogis.

Seconds before the blast, Lucca's voice came out of the blackness and shouted something to Sophia that she did not understand but knew was not good. She felt his hands over her ears just in time as the ground shook and the blast resounded in echoes all around her. Her sweater went to her face filtering out most of the choking dust that followed but not all and she coughed as it touched her throat. As quickly as it happened, all went quiet again and Lucca raised his head. He listened for anything that would signal the intruders were still in the shaft but heard only small stones tumbling occasionally from the ceiling. Satisfied, he turned to Sophia and pulled her to her feet. They descended to the main shaft again and took an eastward direction at a much more leisurely pace. In the welcome light of the relit lantern, Sophia saw that the westerly route was completely blocked by rock and sand.

"We're safe for the moment but I know they weren't caught below it. I saw them running toward the well just after I lit the fuse. We go this way."

Lucca pointed to a dark opening and started for it. The lantern was a very good thing because in just a few steps, the darkness rolled back revealing a gaping hole they would both surely have fallen into without it.

His abrupt stop caused Sophia to bump into him and she let go a little gasp at sight of the deep fissure before them. She recovered and Lucca felt her poke his side jokingly. "Well, this wasn't part of the plan, was it?"

It was clear there would be no jumping or side skirting the cave in. From where they stood it was about a seven to eight feet drop to the secondary cavern floor below and twice the distance across to the other side. The floor of that lower level had also partially collapsed but Lucca could not see what was below it from where he stood.

Lucca checked the rim for soundness then handed Sophia both the light and his pack. He sat down, legs dangling over the edge and slid forward. Lucca smiled at Sophia as he turned slowly around to lower himself onto the narrow ledge below. His plan was good enough. He would slowly touch down on the rock below to test its strength before putting his full weight on it, but a sand covered surface betrayed his grip and Lucca instantly disappeared over the edge.

5 LIKE A DREAM

Sophia screamed and the lantern swung wildly as she dropped to her knees to find Lucca. There on the next ledge down, he lay flat on his back grimacing in pain and Sophia's voice was audibly trembling as she called out to him.

Lucca slowly twisted his back and was relieved to know that he could still move though it was extremely painful. His ears rang and there was a numb feeling at the back of his head that worried him most. His experience with injuries in the past told him that the absence of pain or feeling was usually a sign of something bad. He raised his head and lightly touched the warm bloody gash.

Sophia watched him struggle to sit up and could see the red flow on his collar. Without hesitation, she searched the contents of the knapsack for a bandage and pulled the cloth from around the book. Dust flew as she shook it out before leaning back down and offering it to the dazed Lucca.

"Put this around your head!"

The cloth dropped beside him on the ground and he slowly picked it up and wrapped it around his bleeding scalp. He supposed it a good thing when he pulled it tight and pain shot through the back of his head. The headache and the throbbing quickly replaced the numbness as he staggered to his feet on wobbly legs and over to a large boulder to sit again.

"I'm all right," he finally called back up, but his voice was as shaky as his legs and he slid from the rock and knelt on the floor.

Sophia peered helplessly down at his dazed condition as he remained motionless for the longest time. He sat eyes closed and head spinning without speaking. He was trying very hard to pull himself together and she was relieved to hear him finally speak again.

"I feel fresh air coming from behind me."

Sophia lay over the edge with the lantern keeping watch over him until he finally reopened his down cast eyes and looked around. The haze slowly cleared from his head and under his knees, he noticed something on the floor.

"These are bat droppings. That means there must be an opening somewhere up this passage. It may only be a small one but we might be able to break through enough to get out."

Sophia raised the light toward the other side of the cave in, "But shouldn't we try to get across here first?"

Lucca shook his head, "It's just too far across, for either of us now."

"There has to be a way! We could look for some rope or…" her sentence trailed off as she turned back toward Lucca and saw that his breathing was shallow. He was clearly in more pain than he was telling her.

"Just let me rest for a little. I'll find a way."

His eyes closed again where he knelt and Sophia sat back down and watched him for what seemed like hours that he did not move.

Sophia startled awake from the exhaustion that had overtaken her at the sound of Lucca's voice breaking the long silence.

"Look, look! I need more light down here!"

He himself had drifted in and out of consciousness where he knelt until his body fought off the shock from the fall. His head still felt as though it would burst but his eyes were focused clearly now on a symbol on the wall in front of him. When the full light illuminated it Sophia saw also the drawing was of a bird flying in the direction Lucca had hoped would lead them out.

"It's a different bird but its Cintani art; I know it is!"

"What is the symbol beside it, can you see?" Sophia leaned in as much as she dare and Lucca brushed at the wall with his blood-crusted finger.

"Hand me the book Sophia, hand me the book and hold the light!

Sophia picked up the knapsack and pulled out the old leather. When she had handed it down to Lucca, he held it tightly for a time fighting off dizziness. When it passed he pulled on the cover and there on the inside his eyes found the same symbol. New hope and strength came to him as he looked back to the wall

"It's a cage I think. The same one is here in the book."

Over his shoulder Sophia saw the bird and the short verse below it written in the old language.

"What are the words Lucca? Can you read them?"

Lucca touched the page again and spoke them in Cintani first, then translated on the second pass.

"Fly away with tiny wings
Make your way to light
His hand is there
To loose the door
And keep you safe
In fear's dark flight."

His eyes returned to Sophia and hope rose again. "This bird is flying out the open door, to freedom I think."

Sophia gathered up all their things and put them back into the knapsack. As she handed it down to Lucca, she knew he was aching all over but could do little to help him. They both knew they had to get moving again though neither was sure of the way at all. What Lucca did know was that the Tarantadei would not give up and would return. He also knew they had to get out and warn the others listed in the book. As far as he knew they were safe for the moment, but if any came looking for Sophia and Lucca the Assassin might be waiting and they would be easily picked out as family. This man would likely kill if he even suspected them of being descendants.

Lucca stretched up his arms toward Sophia as she lowered her feet over the ledge.

"I won't let you fall, I promise. Just slide down a little more and I'll have you."

With a deep breath she finally committed herself to his grip around her legs and soon he had lowered her safely to the lower ledge with him. His pain was obvious to her and the added strain had not helped his condition. When he straightened up Sophia turned him around and pulled the bloody bandage away from the wound and inspected his head. It was a nasty gash but the bleeding had slowed from the pressure of the cloth.

"That's a nice whack!"

Lucca responded with a little laugh that he quickly regretted. Pain shot through his ribs and he guessed that one or more was at least cracked but there was little to be done until they could get out and get help.

"Hand me the lantern and look for the birds. Let's get out of here."

Sophia took the pack and Lucca did not protest, as its rubbing would no doubt agitate his ribs. She handed him the lantern and he took a painful step forward. The bat droppings had a strong odor and made the floor slick in places. Each time Lucca's foot would slip, the twisting of his torso was like a knife being plunged into his back. Sophia could see him wince and heard his short labored breathing as he trudged on determined to get them out.

"Just a little farther, do you feel it? The floor is sloping up, we're climbing out!"

"Or further in! You need to rest Lucca, we should stop."

An hour later they were still groping in near darkness. The ground was now dry but his steps were still short and unsure.

"Lucca, you must stop now!" Sophia's small hand on his shoulder felt like a lead weight as he turned and looked into her pleading eyes. "We have heard nothing of them since the explosion, I'm sure it's safe to rest. Please!"

His eyes were glassy from exhaustion and fighting the pain had brought him to at last listen to her. It was Sophia now that helped lower Lucca to the floor as she took the lantern and set it down in front of them. She leaned into the wall herself and pulled him against her as gently as she could. There was little she could do to ease his pain but Sophia tried to make him as comfortable as possible. She felt the rasping in his chest when he pointed to the lantern and spoke.

"We should turn it off."

Sophia reached out to the knob and together they watched the flame shrink to a small glow and then slowly disappear. A moment later, she felt his body relax as unconsciousness claimed him once again. The only sound now was the short in and out breathing that he still fought for in uneasy sleep.

The breeze coming through the cave had steadily become cooler and Sophia pulled her sweater tighter around her neck to stop the chill. She recognized it as the same evening winds that rose and blew in off the sea each night through her bedroom window that now seemed so far away.

She closed her eyes and thought of the soft warm sheets and the fluffy pillow that often wound up on the floor by morning. The cold stone behind her head prompted a promise to herself, that she would appreciate it more the next time she laid her head upon it. She imagined the smell of the fresh picked flowers on the windowsill, filling the room and her dreams with their sweetness. It was as though each flower's fragrance brought a color of its own to the pictures and places she traveled to in wonderful night visions.

Her mother told her that she had always dreamed and remembered in the most vivid manner. It was not that the other children did not dream; it was the details that she brought to the breakfast table that had impressed her family. Her dreams were rarely fragments of an event that day that lingered in her head but specific faces and landscapes she had never seen before.

Even now as she began to doze, brilliant greens and blues were filling her head and streaks of red and yellow were dashed across them creating even more colors where the two crossed over. The perfume in the air and the colors shooting from them intensified, but the flowers she saw were not brightly colored at all. They were the pure white Pamotolea and she was lying in a meadow surrounded by and almost hidden from view amongst them. The breeze rose and warmed slightly, bringing a wave of peace over her that washed away her fears. It was as though she knew the sweet smelling flowers were protecting her from any harm.

Another slight gust arose and without knowing why, she began to softly weep from sadness somewhere deep in her heart. She could not explain it but a realization grew within her that someone had paid a great price for the safety she felt in this place.

Sophia tried to rouse herself from this dream and even managed to raise her heavy eyelids slightly several times, but she was never sure if she was truly awake or not. In either state, the sweet aroma of the small white flowers was now stronger than ever and the colors around them grew brighter.

The seven men stood only yards away in the darkness crushing the flowers and releasing a fine white powder into the breeze that flowed through the shaft. Lucca and Sophia were not aware that they were now covered with the soft silky mist that floated in the darkness.

They had inhaled enough to make them sleep a good long while and when Lucca was lifted from her lap, Sophia's arms fell limp to her sides like a child's rag doll. With tears still streaming down her cheeks, she had a vague sense of gentle hands around her waist but her chin remained on her chest and she at last fully surrendered to the narcotic qualities of the pollen.

Time blurred and the next sensation Sophia had was warmth that covered her whole body. Her eyelids twitched several times as she sat up and opened them to bright sunlight straight over head. There were no more dark cold walls around her, only bright rays framed with tall trees. She stared at the swaying branches above and several minutes passed before her eyes and mind were able to agree on anything.

As the haze in her head continued to clear she came upon the thought of looking about her for something familiar. When that something familiar did come into view, the previous night flooded back in an immediate rush of panic and fear. But relief gently swept in like the next wave on a beach when she saw Lucca's chest rising and falling in unlabored breathing beside her. He slept peacefully, his head wound clean and bandaged and she could see that his ribcage was tightly wrapped with clean linen. His knapsack with the book visible through the opening was at his feet and four apples sat on top. There was also a full wineskin propped against it and a cloth bag full of fresh bread.

Sophia was glad of it but hunger would wait a little longer behind Lucca's well being. Her bruised knees cried out against the pressure as she turned and knelt over him. His face was no longer pained and gray as it had been the night before but slightly flush with color and warm under her fingers. The soft touch stirred him and she regretted disturbing his sleep, but her heart leapt when his eyes fluttered open and looked into hers.

Sunlight behind Sophia splintered through the strands of her hair as Lucca looked up into her smile. He too began to focus on his surroundings with a thousand questions in his mind. Firstly, where they were and then, how they had gotten there. Lucca's voice was a whisper and cracked as he tried to speak. He cleared his dry throat and began again.

"Good morning, I think."

Sophia smiled and laughed softly, but emotion spilled over into her voice as she attempted to answer the casual greeting.

"Morning? It's nearly noon I think! I hope you don't make a habit of sleeping all day!"

The effort to sit up quickly reminded him of his fall in the cave and he rolled to his side and an elbow instead. With Sophia's help, he was able to sit up and look around the woods that surrounded them. His scalp throbbed for a moment before subsiding into a dull ache that ran from the top of his head down to the middle of his back. From there the pain was sharp, short jabs that coincided with any extra deep breath. Sophia picked up the wineskin and offered Lucca a drink.

"I don't remember anything about getting here." Lucca turned toward Sophia waiting to hear her story about the escape but she only shook her head.

Forgetting his thirst, Lucca stared at Sophia, desperately trying to make sense of things as she finally spoke.

"I remember voices in my dream but little more. I was floating and then I was here; this grass beneath my back. There was warmth over me that soaked my skin like a hot fire and I stopped shivering. When the sun woke me up, your head and chest were wrapped."

Sophia held up one of the apples in front of her.

"Who helped us Lucca? Who else knows about this?"

Lucca slowly uncorked the wineskin and took a small taste before deciding the water was safe to drink. After a few swallows he set it aside and his long silence told her that he was more puzzled than she.

"Last night in the cave there *was* someone else there with us; someone with the most amazing eyes. I thought at first that I was just crazy out of my head but He was speaking to me for the longest time."

"What was he saying?"

"I couldn't make out his words really but I knew that he was telling me everything would be fine."

Sophia looked over his head wound again and ventured another question.

"Was it another language?"

"Maybe but, I don't know. He was asking me to do something but I didn't understand; at least I don't think I did. I was afraid at first but the more he spoke the more peace I had and then I just went to sleep."

"That sounds like a dream too Lucca. I had some myself. You should just rest now."

"We didn't dream our way out of that cave Sophia."

Lucca's voice reflected his confusion but Sophia could tell that he wasn't feverish or hallucinating now.

Lucca touched the back of his head lightly and stared at the apple and the bread.

"That thing he was asking me to do…"

Sophia forced a gentle laugh," The one you didn't understand?"

"Yeah," Lucca swallowed hard, "I think I said yes!"

There was little good in throwing more stress into the mix with more unanswerable questions. Instead, Sophia took a bite of the apple and savored the sweet juice filling her mouth. It brought hunger back to the forefront and she pulled a loaf of bread from the bag and handed it to Lucca. He ripped some off and both took a piece.

The battered young man watched Sophia pull the one book from his knapsack and hold it with both hands. After a moment she drew a deep breath and split the pages as though she expected something frightening to happen. It opened to the center and below a drawing of a fierce beast were the strange markings of the old writing. Lucca peered over her shoulder and quietly began reciting the words in the old tongue. As he spoke, Sophia felt a stirring of something deep within her like an urgent calling to remember her part in something long past. She touched the words on the page and searched for the memories.

"I know this! I don't know what you're saying but I've heard these words before.

What does it say Lucca, what is this?"

"Funny, that you should pick this one. This was my first pick out of all of these too. It's the writing of an ancient poet. He lived during the darkest times of Cintani."

Sophia turned and handed Lucca the book.

"Then you know what it says! Tell me what he says. Please?"

Lucca studied the verse a moment and then began translating.

"The people lived in fear,
For there was no one there
Strong enough to fight the dragon
And end his reign of death.
The old ones told of one
Who came so very long ago
And took away the dragon's power,
But how could that be so?
For the dragon still could plunder
And make our hearts grow weak,

Then another of the old ones slowly stood to speak.
The power of the dragon
Is not power of his own,
The power belonged to someone else,
Though very few have known.
"Then who" we cried,
Has given back the dragon of their might?
If he has given, he must take it back!
He must fight!"

There was more but Lucca's head had begun to spin slightly and he felt sick for just a moment. When he closed the book and handed it back to Sophia, she took it to her chest like a strange new treasure. She held it there for the longest time as though the words were soaking into her soul.

Lucca looked out toward the sound of the sea, inhaling the air and the moistness of it felt welcome in his dusty lungs.

"I think the book really found me when I was still fishing and looking for something else. After the day's nets were put away and the men were playing cards, I would sit on the stern and watch the stars appear over the water. That's when I would hear those old phrases echoing around in my head and see my grandfather's face. Sometimes he would be in my dreams too. We would be off on some great adventure that made no sense, but was all the same very exciting. Maybe I first went back looking to find some part of him again. I didn't expect or want any of this."

Sophia took in his words for a moment then leaned into him.

"I have always dreamed without answers but knew someday I would find them. They frighten me now but I know I have to hear them. I have to know more."

They broke more of the fresh bread and found the remaining cheese in his knapsack to be slightly dusty but a very much welcome addition to their late breakfast. Lucca finally stood and walked the area looking for landmarks.

"By the sun and the wind, I'm sure we are on the other side of the island from the tower. That looks like the back of the crater there through the trees. But it would have taken us a full day to walk here from there! For us to be here, the passage would have to come straight through the mountain."

In the distance Lucca had already heard the surf pounding on the rocky eastern coast, which further convinced him of their position. He scanned the area for tracks but the only places that the grass lay over was from the moving about they had done since waking up.

"I think we can easily walk to Orani from here. I have a friend there that will keep you safe for a while. I can take the ferry back around to home and when it's safe, I'll send for you."

Orani was a small fishing village on the opposite side of the island from Lucca and Sophia's home. The mainland ferry would run first to there, then down around the cliffs of Imanado to the south, around the point and up to Kerdaino. From there it would return to Orani and then back to the mainland. There was little north of Orani worth seeing. There was one small cove northward but it was open to the rough sea in the winter and the black shifting sands were always changing the bottom of the inlet. A boat of any size could easily be foundered and risk of capsizing in the high waves was great.

Sophia wanted to be happy but her stomach twisted knowing that it would not be that simple. She said nothing then but her thoughts were deep and kept to herself for most of the walk to the sea.

6 ALDO

The old dog barked half-heartedly but never bothered to get up as Lucca and Sophia climbed the hill to the old house surrounded by lobster pots and draped in fishing nets. By the time they reached the fence around the yard, a heavyset man with a scowl on his unshaven face appeared in the open doorway. He rubbed his hand over his beard and unkempt hair, looking like he'd just been interrupted from a nap.

Aldo could not see to write his name without his glasses but the eyes that could see a minnow flash across the bay saw quickly that it was his old friend moving slowly toward him and he was not well. Faster than Sophia thought him able, Aldo was over to them and had Lucca by the arm as he eyed her and the road behind them suspiciously.

Aldo was a good friend to Lucca and they had often helped each other find good catch even in lean seasons. When Aldo became sick, Lucca went out of his way to keep his men fishing and handled all the repairs on his boat through those months.

Aldo in turn, provided Lucca with port if ever seas became too angry to return around the island safely. He would house and feed his whole crew if necessary until the weather passed. Lucca needed this safe port now more than ever and knew he could trust his good friend for secrecy as well.

"Blast it Boy; what happened to you?"

Lucca grinned weakly and put his hand on Aldo's, his voice calm and matter of fact,

"Too big a fish story to tell here in the yard, but give us a chair and I'll tell you all about it!"

Aldo let out a guarded little chuckle that was cut short by another quick look at Sophia. It seemed that he feared this was her doing and didn't know how much to say in front of her. But his concern for his friend brushed that aside and he led them on to the house.

Inside, a cat was unceremoniously knocked from the table and Aldo pulled the chair out for Lucca. Eyes still on his injured friend, he simply pointed Sophia to another chair and went to the cupboard for some glasses. He returned and filled them from a dark green bottle. The deep purple liquid slopped over the sides as he fired a series of questions at Lucca.

"Where is the Casone? Did you anchor off shore? How did you get here?" Lucca took the first cup and handed it to Sophia.

"She's safe enough at home. Sophia and I hoped that you might help answer how we got here."

Aldo frowned again and began in a disgusted tone,

"If you got drunk and don't remember man, how am

I supposed to? Looks like you got in some fight though!"

He glanced at Sophia again and then back to Lucca, "Was it over her?"

A look from Lucca told Aldo that as his habit, he had over stepped his boundaries and he sat back a much quieter man. He spoke to the table struggling to keep his tone as polite as was in the crusty fisherman.

"Sorry if I said somethin, I'm just not used to seeing friends all busted up for no reason."

From there, Lucca began by telling Aldo that the tales he'd called ghost stories and drunkard's lies had taken flesh and were loose somewhere on the island. He laid out the danger of the Tarantadei and what might happen.

"I have to go back to Kerdaino and talk to everyone. I want you to take care of Sophia for me."

Aldo sat shaking his head," Say this guy *is* looking for you; you'll get spotted with your bandages sure thing! And look at you; you're in no shape to take on a man anyway. Stay here till you're stronger."

Lucca's voice quieted but his resolve was firm as he pulled at the white gauze on his head.

"That's no good! Now he is sure that Cintani blood still exists here and may already have found a name. I have to go."

Sophia put down her glass and added a third option.

"I should go!"

Aldo jerked his head in her direction and the first real smile Sophia had seen since their arrival spread across his face. "Yea, send her!"

Again, Lucca glared at his opinionated friend and shook his head. Aldo returned his eyes to the table but

Sophia's voice and her own resolve rose,

"I can ride with the tourists on the ferry much easier than you and he won't be looking for a woman."

Lucca twisted on his chair and pain shot through his ribcage again. Aldo decided to sit this one out, arms folded across his broad chest.

Sophia lowered her voice, "Tell us what to say to convince your family and then together we can warn all the families."

Aldo's eyes rose to her in surprise and his arms unfolded, "We?"

7 BACK TO KERDAINO

There was nothing Lucca liked about this plan. He hated being in this pain and he hated the idea of Sophia returning without him but Aldo promised that he would take care of her.

"You just be careful with my boat," he said as he patted the big sleepy dog on its head.

Sophia laughed, "Do we have to carry him or can he stand on his own?"

Aldo walked to the door and whistled. The big dog sprang up, shook himself and then trotted straight out into the yard.

Lucca was oblivious to their taunting of each other. He was stocking his knapsack as he barked orders.

"When you get there, make sure you aren't followed, then go straight to your house. Aldo will speak to my family; you get your mother to where the Casone is tied. Speak to as few people as possible."

Sophia wrapped the warm wool blanket around her shoulders and adjusted the kerchief on her head.

"We'll be fine; it's you that needs to be careful!"

Lucca rattled on, "When it gets dark I'll dock the Cristiana beside the Casone and be able to look the docks over for strangers. The Tarantadei looks for us to come back down the coast from the north. I doubt he will notice when I dock from the south. Bring everyone down to the cannery as quietly as you can so we can talk about what to do next."

Aldo nodded as he touched Sophia's arm and gently nudged her toward the gate.

"We should go if we want to catch the last ferry tonight. Don't worry Lucca, we'll take her safe."

The quietness in his voice was the first sign of his soft heart that Sophia had glimpsed since they arrived and a feeling of repentance for the way she'd thought of him welled up in her. As they turned away from Lucca and set out toward the ferry, she considered that perhaps he was just hiding his own pain behind this gruffness. After a few extra long strides to catch up with him, she heard him speaking and strained to hear what he was mumbling to himself.

"Don't know how I got into this, there's no good in a woman's help! No Sir, I should have set the dog on them when they came up the road!"

"You just better do your part when we get there," She snapped, "that's all I can say!"

Aldo, slowed to a stop and his shoulders sagged under the burden of now trying to smooth things over with a half-hearted apology of some sort. Sophia however, stormed past and down the hill, being sure to give him no opportunity. He took breath as to call after her but judged that it would be a useless effort and let it go in a heavy sigh. Even Leviathan deserted him and trotted off following Sophia's quick march. His feet picked up again and he trudged on after them toward the ferry dock.

Aldo and Sophia sat a small distance apart on the ferry and pretended not to know each other but there was never a moment she was out of his site. Many people of course knew Aldo but his reputation as a sour old fisherman insured that no one asked him his business that night.

He pulled his smelly old fishing knife from his belt and much to Sophia's disgust, sat carving chunks from an apple. Occasionally, he would let go a loud belch as he wiped the blade clean on the front of his coat. He noted in a passing glance her disapproval of his manners and after turning his face to the sea, enjoyed a light chuckle. His amusement was cut short however by a voice he knew and dreaded.

The wife of old man Polani was quick to stick her nose in everyone's business and he cringed as he listened to her subtle interrogation.

"What brings you to be traveling alone so late in the day young lady?"

Sophia turned toward the old woman beside her and tried to calm her pounding heart. Out of the corner of her eye, she could see Aldo making a slashing motion across his throat along with his usual scowl.

Clearing her throat, Sophia smiled back,

"Excuse me?"

The old woman wagged a bony finger at her and shook her head. "Young ladies in my day were never allowed to travel alone. We always had an escort! People wonder about a girl that travels alone. Now you just come right over here and I'll make sure that you are not bothered by any unpleasant sorts!"

Sophia probably should have said something else but she didn't. With the same sweet smile she looked straight at the proper lady and fired,

"Perhaps you should wonder about a girl like me!" Sophia looked down and patted Leviathan's broad head and his tail wagged lazily across the deck. When her eyes returned to Mrs. Polani, she had reloaded,

"Thank you but I rather prefer the company I boarded with."

Mrs. Polani's smile was no more and Sophia watched the disgruntled busy body whirl in a huff of indignation and storm away to the other side of the boat. Aldo's eyes were wide but his big toothy smile was wider and he wondered why he hadn't been able to be rid of the meddling old woman that easily.

Time passed slowly for Lucca as Aldo's boat; the Cristiana shadowed the ferry toward their homeport. His mind was full of urgent tasks and he bemoaned the injuries that had forced him to delegate them to Sophia and his friend. As the sun disappeared, the lights of the ferry were lit and he watched them bobbing up and down in the mild sea. He scanned the horizon for other vessels but happily saw none for most boats were by this time of day tucked safely in their birth or far out to sea.

The hour run around the island was finally over and his home harbor was now in sight. The ferry docked and there was the usual crowd milling about waiting for packages or loved ones returning from the mainland. Both Aldo and Sophia scanned the faces for anyone or thing that looked out of place. She heard Aldo's voice behind her as they waited for the gangplank to be lowered.

"Stay in the crowd as long as you can before you

make for home. I'll follow just out of sight for a bit. You'll be fine."

With a "thud," the ramp was in place and the passengers began moving ashore. The crowd moved slowly but eventually reached the end of the dock and the main street. As they began to disperse Sophia saw that she was left standing in the open and moved to the sidewalk. So began the walk in and out of shadows toward her home on the edge of the bay.

Lucca and Sophia's Mothers had been close friends and the children had grown up in houses that were very close together. The mothers had in fact, grown up in the very same houses and their parents were good friends. All had left home for a short time but came back to the island eventually and the families stayed quite close.

Lucca's Mother Tatiana had a sister named Ludwena who married and lived down the coast a few miles south of the tower and inland. When Lucca's father disappeared at sea, Ludwena and her husband Yauvot helped Tatiana a great deal with the wild little man she had been left to raise on her own. Lucca spent much time with his aunt and uncle and Yauvot taught him a little of farming and even some about fishing. His mother wanted to keep him far from the fishing lanes so it was of course very hard on her when he chose his father's profession and took to the sea that had taken her husband.

Sophia's mother Thaliana had been a seamstress and her husband a farmer with land on the Imanado. Both family homes were just out of town to the east but when Sophia's father passed, her mother moved them into town and bought a two story along the coast a short distance from the harbor. She took in sewing from there and actually did much better. With more walk in business and a central location, she was able to send Sophia off to school on the mainland. Sophia's grades were good but she somehow could not find her place in the big world and had returned home to rest and ponder her future.

Tatiana also moved into town and her brother moved back from the mainland when Lucca grew up and left for the big world beyond the island. When Lucca returned and bought his own boat, the three of them worked together to sell Lucca's fish. His mother handled the payroll for his crew and his uncle helped with the maintenance of the Casone.

Both families kept the old homes and rented them out as vacation homes for a number of years and then eventually sold them to young families wanting to escape mainland life. There had been hard times to be sure but in all it was a good life they lived. In this pocket of peace just off the beaten track most of the world's ills passed them by. They continued on here as their parents had for the most part unnoticed and content to be so.

Now, the usually cheery street was filled with shadowy shapes and the corners she'd walked a thousand times were dangerous open spaces she hoped to cross without being noticed. She glanced behind her but Aldo was nowhere to be seen which increased her sense of aloneness.

She was glad when her house came in sight but a sense of dread rose within her at the same time. Sophia walked on past checking both sides of the street for anyone that might be lurking nearby. All looked peaceful but her heart still raced and told her to beware. It was only a day past that all was happy here and as far as Sophia knew, her mother had just put the cat out and turned to her evening sewing.

At the alley between the two story buildings she paused before slipping into the dark and the rear door of her home. She quietly turned the handle and held her breath. The bolt clicked from the striker so loud she was sure the whole town had heard it. It was of course only a small snap but she froze and listened. Hearing nothing, the door was pushed open and the light from the kitchen spilled out into the alley.

The big dog sniffed briefly at the opening then lumbered inside and began to explore. Sophia waited and listened a moment more before having enough nerve to follow, for it was not right that the rest of the house should be so dark this early in the evening.

Sophia stepped in and inched slowly across the empty kitchen where the dinner plates still sat unused on the table. The cold stove and empty pots put her heart in her throat. Leviathan had found the cat dish and with noisy slurps made short work of the few morsels left there. His lack of stealth irritated Sophia but she was still glad of him being there as she peered around the door casing to the dark family room. The room contained only empty chairs and the big soft couch where her mother's sewing still lay in the usual heap of swatches and thread spools. She looked to the stairs and worked on her courage again. Her lungs drew in the air and her lips began forming words, but they came out as barely more than a whisper.

"Mamma, are you here?'

Scampering back into the kitchen she turned and waited for an answer but it was never given. "Mamma, where are you?

Sophia's voice was louder now as she again ventured out of the kitchen to the stairs that led to the bedrooms. Moonlight from the window at the end of the upstairs hall streamed uninterrupted like a silver river to a waterfall. But instead of cascading down each of the steps Sophia stood on, it weightlessly floated straight on, into a brilliant puddle of light against the living room wall above her head.

She was watching fragments of dust float and swirl with the currents above when she suddenly felt herself begin to float and spin as well. Sophia became so dizzy that a fear of falling came over her and she quickly sat down and gripped the banister. It was there in that light river that the bits of dust slowly pulled together into the shape of tiny ships sailing up and away.

Blinking and rubbing did nothing to erase them from her eyes and in wonder; she reached out as a child for a firefly. Like the insect, they gracefully eluded her each time and sailed on to disappear at the end of the light. It was so strange to be feeling this way at this time but her heart was suddenly light. A pleasant smile crossed her lips for circumstance and time seemed to cease until the last ship dissolved into darkness.

Reality finally bounded past her and up the staircase as Leviathan nearly bowled her over. Sophia refocused on the big dog's claws tapping across the wood floor as he sniffed from room to room. His big nose and keen eyes gave him no reason to growl or bark and assured Sophia that no one waited there. The dizziness was gone and when her hand touched the top post of the banister, the dog was just coming out of the furthest bedroom. He trotted up to her and then back into another room with no particular concern for any area.

Sophia followed him in and looked for some reason that everyone would be gone but there seemed to be absolutely nothing out of place. The beds were made the way that Mamma always did every morning and the big fluffy pillows sat just right up against the headboards.

Her room-to-room search ended with her sitting on her own bed staring at the flowers by the window. Except for Sophia's clean and folded laundry on the dresser, the room looked exactly the way she had left it. What to do now was heavy on her mind and she turned to the dog as if he had an opinion.

"Now what do we do? Where did they go?"

Leviathan nuzzled into her hands and she pulled gently on his big ears. The dog offered no solution and soon wandered off and down the stairs.

8 NEW FRIENDS

A clean sweater sounded like a good idea to Sophia so she went to the closet to pick one. She was cold on the ferry and thought another blanket would be very welcome in the night mist too. Just as thoughts and hand touched the quilt, a quiet voice broke the silence and fear struck her like an ocean wave.

"Sophia."

She whirled around to flee but a tall figure in the doorway blocked her escape. "You needn't worry about your mother, she is safe."

A man's voice flowed like an old river; deep and calm and when his eyes met hers, Sophia felt his confidence touch her from across the room. Just the same, she edged toward the window and another exit. The stranger made no attempt to stop her.

Sophia realized that he was even taller that she first thought. He would have had to stoop a great deal to enter the doorway and his shoulders might have brushed either side as he passed through. His olive green armor under a full-length cloak made Sophia stare. It was as though one of the soldiers painted on the wall of the tunnels had peeled off the painting and came to life here in her room.

Her light-headedness returned as she flashed back to her dizzy spell and the ships in the stairway.

"Where is my mother," Sophia said taking another unsteady step toward the windowsill, "and who are you? Are you really here?"

The soldier grinned. "I am Daenos; I have come to take you to safety also. You must come now for the Sandosu is about to begin."

Sophia was wondering what a Sandosu was and if she could make it out the window before he could grab her.

Daenos continued. "The Tarantadei now know of this place and we must be gone from it. I will take you to your mother."

Her hand now touched the window latch but still he did not move.

"How do I know you're not a Tarantadei? Why should I trust you?"

Sophia was wondering how she would jump to the street without breaking her neck when the old dog found his way back and trotted up to this stranger like an old friend. Daenos stooped and rubbed the big ears of the tail wagging Leviathan and Sophia puzzled at how unconcerned either one was with her movements.

Daenos pushed back his cloak as he rubbed the dog's belly and the sleeve of his long, loose fitting shirt rode up his arm. There, Sophia saw a tattooed image she had only seen hours before but recognized instantly. It was a small but unmistakable Cintani bird. Daenos finally looked up and spoke again, "What does your heart tell you?"

Aldo had stood in a dark doorway watching Sophia and Leviathan make their way up the street. When finally she was out of sight he pulled his cap down tight and padded quietly down the stone street in the direction that Lucca lived.

They had reasoned that a woman would not be suspect but even though he saw no one behind Sophia, Aldo still wished that they had stayed together. He had never taken much stock in the stories Lucca had told him and even now was hardly a believer. But he did believe in his friend and if he thought there was something so wrong Aldo was more than willing to help him sort it all out. He moved from block to block without sound like an alley cat; seeing but not being seen by the sleeping village around him. There was a faster, more direct route but Aldo knew that the extra minute or two gave him much more cover.

When at last he arrived, the house looked empty from his scrutiny over the stone wall at the back door. It troubled something in him to see the home of his friend so dark and quiet tonight. There were few places in this time of his life that he had felt the freedom to be himself more than at Lucca's home.

It was a place where he could simply relax and laugh along with the family that so easily took him by the arm and set him at their table. The warmth of the good food and the good hearts melted away his defenses and he knew that no one judged him for his life's mistakes. Instead, he felt a surge of hope for himself and always left with an old song on his mind and a smile amid his whiskers.

Tonight, he was careful not to be seen as he crossed the yard lit by moonlight and pressed his back against the wall beside the window. He felt no vibrations in it and heard no sound to indicate movement inside at all. Slowly, he edged toward the dirty windowpane to venture a glimpse at the dark room. He squinted into the darkness but saw little beside his own reflection in the glass and the moon behind him.

Like Sophia's house, the rear door opened into the kitchen and like most of the houses here, had no lock. He quietly twisted the handle and pushed it open ever so slowly. A time or two it creaked and each time he paused to listen for a reaction from inside. When it was wide enough for him to fit through, he crouched down and slipped inside to the dark corner behind it and listened again. The old wood floor was sure to creak if anyone was moving about but all was quiet.

From his corner he could see the front door and the sliver of light between it and the frame. He stood and quietly worked his way around the wall to the entrance and found that it had not been forced open as he had first thought but possibly left ajar by those leaving in a hurry. A glove on the floor a short distance inside and an empty coat rack furthered his theory that the house was indeed deserted quickly.

Aldo scratched his whiskered chin and looked for more answers. Upstairs he found nothing out of place and there were no signs of struggle anywhere. When Lucca's uncle and mother went out the front door they were doing so under their own power and it did not appear to be against their will. But where did they go and why would they leave unless they thought there was in fact some danger?

Stepping to the front porch he tried to imagine the events of the evening but none of it made sense. The moon rose higher and in the distance he heard the breakers growing louder. It told the old seaman that soon it would be high tide. An old gray cat sauntered up the porch steps to rub against his leg and he unconsciously bent and scooped it up in his arms. He scratched its tattered ears and tried to think over the loud purring.

"You have a good heart; he senses it."

The voice behind him though steady and quiet hit Aldo like a foghorn and for the second time today a cat was launched from a place of comfort. His knife was out in a flash as he whirled about to face the tall shadow but just as quickly the stranger's steel flashed and Aldo's blade went flying.

9 REUNION

Lucca chugged the Christiana into the harbor just moments after the ferry without notice since there was so much commotion with everyone trying to get off. He cut the engine and guided the old fishing boat smoothly into the extra slip at the old dock in front of the cannery and shut off all the lights. The Casone sat quietly in the next birth and Lucca imagined his boat glad to see him though no light shone from her windows and all was quiet. He scanned her deck for anything out of place before judging it safe to step to the dock between them and secure the Cristiana. With that done, he boarded the Casone and crept toward the cabin that looked to be as he left it. He swept the deck and interior with his eyes a second time and a small relief came that the plan might really work.

The door slid quietly open and he was sure that no one had seen him go in, but just in case he reached down to the side of the small cabinet and found his fishing knife. There had been several occasions that just having it strapped it to his side averted larger arguments with larger men that drank too much. Both then and now his hope was to leave it where it was.

He sat in the dark of the cabin, binoculars in hand and eventually, where the crowd thinned at the bottom of the ramp, a familiar old dog trotted into sight. He raised the glasses and watched the silhouette of a young woman looking in all directions as she left the docks along the south road. Leviathan made a wide circle before falling in behind her, sniffing the ground here and the air there as he followed up the street. Aldo appeared shortly thereafter and Lucca watched him slip away smoothly in the same direction. He was encouraged as he scanned the area and saw nothing suspicious but now all he could do was wait and hope that they would return soon.

The light night fog that filled harbor and crowded the docks seemed especially eerie tonight; maybe because Lucca wished he could see the whole harbor without its veil or maybe because his eyes were so clouded with fatigue. Either way, he was having a hard time staying awake now as there in the dark, the boat moved gently back and forth between the lines with the small swells that entered the harbor. He had spent many nights like this while fishing and he wished now that he had his nets down in that favorite bay southwest of here. The blanket around his shoulders was warm and dry and the sounds of the sea at night were always mysterious but peaceful to him.

His eyes nearly shut before he shook himself and shifted positions. Sitting up straighter for a while but gradually sinking back against the bulkhead, he was exhausted from his injuries and the trip. His eyes burned from diesel fumes and being open much too long again. Pressing them tightly shut for a moment gave relief for a little while but each time he closed them it was harder to raise the heavy lids back up.

He fought hard against it but reality and dreams soon merged and he was unaware that the latter had taken over completely. His head flopped to one side and his body relaxed in deepening slumber despite the visions of watchfulness he perceived as true.

All was to him as though he had suddenly been refreshed and he found his feet standing on the bow, again scanning the harbor town. The docks were tranquil and the high evening fog circled the streetlights giving each a silvery aura round about. The buoy bell clanged softly at the mouth of the bay and somewhere across the docks gulls quarreled loudly over a scrap of fish. All seemed quite peaceful to him and he struggled to remember the reason that he was not home by a crackling fire on a cold night like this one.

Then, out of the night came a figure along the wooden plank walk leading to the cannery moorage. From far away the tall man in long unfamiliar style of cloak stepped slowly but deliberately toward the Casone. The unmistakable shape of olive green armor spread across his broad chest and abdomen. His loins were girded with thick leather and his boots of like material rose high on is calves.

Lucca watched him in this dream without concern until he reached the gangplank of the boat and stood looking deep into Lucca's eyes. There was something fearful about him but Lucca was not afraid, even when the stranger stepped on board and stood towering over him. His expression was solemn and his voice seemed full of meaning beyond the words he spoke.

"You have opened the door to your destiny and to those of your line. Long we have waited for the awakening of truth in our land and now you must find the strength within the book of ages to defeat the lies of the past."

Lucca cocked his head and listened like one who had heard these words and this voice before. Flashes of faces appeared in his mind and a vague memory of being lifted and carried from darkness to the bright sun.

"Remember the old poet's words; about the Dragon? Remember the last of the verse?"

Lucca thought back to the words he had been translating to Sophia. The lines he had not finished came to him.

"The power was your own He said

But through your fear and doubt,

You've listened to the dragon's lies

And trickery won out.

Here is the sword you need

To take the power that he took,

But confusion filled our hearts and minds,

For the old one held a book.

The dragon is a roaring beast

That hasn't any teeth,

And the words within this leather book

Are swords within a sheath.

Take the word of Elyan

Slay your dragon now,

Know the truth and He will make you free."

The man's cloak fell back revealing the full garb of the warrior beneath. The ornate hilt of a huge sword was visible at the top of a long metal sheath and his large hand rested on the end of the grip. It was a menacing blade but what drew Lucca's eye was the ring on his finger above it. Forgetting all else, he was drawn to stare at the circle of flame and the bird that flew within. It was Cintani yes, but not the frightened little sparrow from the caves. It was to him defiant and fearsome and no longer fleeing from the hunter. It somehow imparted strength and hope to Lucca just by looking upon it.

"Arise my friend, we have a journey to make and battle to prepare for. We must indeed, make for that favorite bay. The high cliffs behind it will shield us from strangers at our back. "

Light flashed off of the ring and Lucca blinked from the brightness. He blinked again and realized that he was no longer on the bow but once again, slumped over in the cabin. But the warrior's ring still flashed in his eyes as he leaned over Lucca and pointed to the one book on the table beside them.

"Arise now, for it is time we take our kin to a safer landfall."

Lucca's head jerked back against the hull as he startled awake and the gash on the back of his head began to throb anew. Scrambling to his feet, he clutched the old fishing knife at his side and struggled to drive the fog from his head. The man continued to point at the book but made no attempt to take it as Lucca gathered himself up and grasped it with his free hand. The ring was not a dream, nor the feeling that something was unexplainably good in and about his guest.

"Do not fear me; I am Banda of the Naarai. We are keepers of the one book and Elyan is for you." It was at those words that Lucca later told everyone that his head stopped throbbing. The headache faded away almost completely and from that moment forward it became increasingly easier to breathe. His head gash was still very much there and tender but now only to the touch.

"We are here to see you to safety. Look and see the others coming! Assure them that they too will be safe!"

Lucca's eyes followed the ring and at the end of the stranger's waved hand he could see a line of familiar village faces streaming slowly out of the dark. With each of the small family groupings came an armed guard just like the one that stood beside him now.

None of this made any sense and Lucca was pretty sure that one or both people on the Casone right now had lost touch with reality. His sensibility told him not to trust someone with a sword nearly as tall as he, yet here was more help than he could have imagined.

Banda moved out on deck and Lucca followed; still cautiously watching his odd but apparent ally. The soldier's prompting told him that there was no time to change the plan and so far there seemed no good reason to. He would go with it for now and reasoned that if things went wrong the assemblage as a whole could possibly overpower these few men. On deck however, Lucca reassessed the man's stature and became less optimistic about a rebellion. Banda grinned as if he knew and was amused by Lucca's thoughts.

"We are for you Lucca," Banda repeated as the approaching soldiers responded in like to his upraised hand.

Joy and urgency mixed as Lucca greeted his family and neighbors directing them on board one boat or the other. Each carried something like an armload of blankets or a basket of bread. Some had boxes of vegetables or fish but all looked as though they had left their homes without much notice. All were as fearful of what lay ahead of them as what might be behind. When Lucca hugged his mother and uncle he promised her that he would tell them all about this later but for now he needed her to help with the others. Later she would tell him the story of how they had been brought here. About the dreams she had had of the very soldier who appeared in the house to warn them just as the sun was setting.

His uncle told of the stranger he met in the bait shop and the questions about old things he had almost forgotten. All there had some tale of an ill feeling that had arrived among them in the past few days that they could not explain. Everyone had a healthy fear of these strangely clothed men and hesitated in coming but an even stronger sense of urgency to heed their warning had led them here to the docks. It was like something had awakened in these, the last families of the Cintani and called them to believe again. Lucca realized this might have been very much the feelings of the ancient Cintani people fleeing from death by Roman sword.

It was plain that these silent sentinels had far out paced his plan as the list of Cintani names in Lucca's head had now assembled on the docks. The two people that he wanted to see most however were still not there and he worried that something had happened.

"They are not forgotten and you will see them soon." Banda's big hand on his shoulder was heavy but the calm resolve on the warrior's face gave hope to Lucca's heart. Lucca could see over Banda's shoulder to the mouth of the harbor and the sea beyond. He had picked several destinations but was not truly confident about any of them. He had seen first hand that even the mainland was not safe.

Banda followed Lucca's thoughtful gaze to the open water.

"It will be our friend tonight good captain; I know you will bring us through without loss. I can see the wisdom of the book in you. Look to it to help you now for there is much you can do that you do not realize."

Lucca twisted his sore neck and touched the back of his head.

"It was one thing to read the book with my grand father; now I'm really not sure I ever want to open it again."

"That is wisdom Lucca, for it is both great and terrible.

Lucca lifted his head to look at Banda, "You take it and use it!

Banda's eyes burned on Lucca now, "I can hold it safe for a short season but it has fallen to you my friend to speak from it. You are of the Cintani bloodline and the finder of the one book. While it is on the move we may bear it but it was never for us to wield; only to protect."

At his summons, Daenos appeared and Lucca handed him the old book.

"It will be always within your reach as it should be. The Naarai are glad of your rising and serve you now."

Lucca watched Daenos tuck the book under the breastplate of his green armor and his spirit felt the warrior's solemn, unspoken vow to guard it ferociously. What had been a list of names appeared now to be much more important than he had ever dreamed. There were so many questions without answers and now he wasn't sure he wanted to find them.

That familiar bark rang across the harbor and Lucca looked to see the old dog trotting down the planks toward him. A moment later his eyes followed a movement in the fog and Sophia and Aldo appeared with a Naarai soldier leading and another warrior close behind.

"You see Lucca," Banda said, "My friend Daenos has

brought them safe."

Lucca left any heaviness behind and made his way toward them where there was a glad reunion. Sophia had no words but rushed into Lucca's open arms with no intention of letting go any time soon.

Aldo's voice was gruff as usual but his handshake was indication that he was glad to see his old friend again.

"You didn't tell me you invited your own army to this party! I would have just as soon known a little more before they scared ten years out of me."

Lucca gazed back at the crowd. He counted seven of these Naarai warriors now moving silently among the people. All were huge, fierce looking men and not one face showed the slightest hint of fear. In fact, there was a strange peace that came over anyone that made eye contact.

"They seem to have invited themselves Aldo and it's looking like it was a good thing."

Banda was not quite a giant, but very tall and very battle ready to Lucca's mind.

"It's time, we must go now."

By the time Lucca and Aldo had the engines running, the soldiers had all come aboard and cast off the lines. The fishing boats pulled back from the dock and Lucca looked to Banda.

"So where do you think we should go?"

"We must go toward the cliffs of Imanado, do you know them?"

"Yes, but…"

"Time is close but they are a good distance behind us. Make for the shadows of the great wall."

Banda's confidence was persuasive so the discussion seemed to be over for the moment. The Casone led out of the harbor and both boats soon disappeared into the night beyond it. A safe distance from the rocks along the coastline Lucca turned to port and angled toward Imanado. The fog thinned and the moon rose almost full but Lucca and Aldo would have known blindfolded almost exactly where they were. They could see in their mind's eye every rock and dock that jutted out from the very familiar coastline. Lucca also knew the cliffs and knew that there was no safety or hiding at their destination.

He reasoned that Banda meant to lead them to Orani where there was shelter from the sea and the point would provide a good lookout for anyone approaching.

"There's really nothing there you know, I mean there's no good sheltering at all there."

Banda seemed unconcerned.

"I trust you, and you must begin to trust me."

10 BALIN

Balin emerged from the smoking well still cursing and coughing. He was covered in dust and his face was twisted with rage as he made his way back to the main road and the old truck that Pogis had acquired the previous day. His fingers twisted the key violently several times before the engine grudgingly awoke with loud groaning and smoke. Another thrust shoved it in gear and gravel flew as he pulled on the lights and hit the main road.

He wiped his face and spit angrily out the window at the island that had tried to swallow him up and the old truck careened wildly down the road back toward town. He was now sure that the Cintani were still on this rock and now that they knew of him there was no doubt in his mind that they would try to run like rabbits. But they tried to escape him before and none had succeeded. He could hide in the shadows better than most and sooner or later these frightened little rabbits would crawl out of their holes and he would be there.

The truck was abandoned a street away from his motel and Balin walked through the evening gray to his room and locked the door behind him.

"You have underestimated this rabbit and your arrogance has cost you your concealment.

Balin felt the snake shaped scars on his neck begin to burn and turned with a sneer toward the blackness that spoke to him.

"I have lost little besides the maggot Pogis that gave me information too late. You can be sure, Great Rajir; I will not fail!"

"Your doggedness is worthless to me now for you are already too late to kill the heirs of the Cintani here. My spies have brought word that they already have been secreted away and have protectors that you cannot face alone. Now there are greater events unfolding and you must listen to me carefully and not fail again! I am summoning all the forces of the Darjan to this place for a final battle is soon to be. Know that I will invade their secret lands and crush them!"

Fierce hatred rose up in Balin and his eyes glazed over at the humiliating words that were spit at him. With his fists clenched, he fought hard against it but the black presence forced him slowly to his knees in a bow of submission. He could not speak for the tightness in his throat and pain in his chest. He felt the arrogance of the blackness as it held him down.

"Now go to the village and find the drunken sea captain that brought you here. He will take you to the black sands and you will give my general my instructions. Do not disappoint me in this little thing Balin. I tire of your bumbling."

When the pain lifted the darkness had also dissolved and he picked up the sealed parchment lying at his feet. He cursed again and thought of how he hated being on the sea. No matter how calm the water, a morbid fear of it always rose in him without reason.

Since he chose to partner with Rajir it also gripped him in terrible dreams. Steely fingers from the black depths would pull him under as he fought to hold his breath. He would struggle on for seeming hours before the precious bubbles of air would finally burst from his lungs and swirl away upwards in front of his eyes. His lungs burned as the urge to inhale the dark water would be too much to hold off any longer. The panic was blinding as he thrashed wildly to escape certain death. At that moment he would wake up gasping and gulping at the air around his bed, drenched in cold sweat as though he had indeed just been plucked from the depths. Even when the nightmare had passed, he would lean sullen against the headboard and deny himself anymore sleep that night.

Fear controlled him but also fueled his hatred and ambition. He despised this master but at the same time aspired to brandish the same level of poisonous evil in his being. It was this hunger that drew him in and convinced him to ignore the obvious danger for the sake of fanatical power.

The old salt of a boat captain seemed to be waiting for Balin as he padded down the dock and onto the rusty-hulled vessel. They were quickly on their way but the age and condition of the old boat made it move slowly. Balin tried to sleep but he could not for there were always memories floating in and out of his dreams as he tossed back and forth. So much so that he never really felt like he slept at all anymore. He was just a touch of paranoia away from ever fully relaxing and no amount of alcohol could make the haunting whispers fully dissipate.

They started so long ago that he most likely could not remember the young boy that knew nothing of war and hatred. It plagued him that he had no memories of his mother and only fleeting glimpses of a hard and demanding father. When he closed his eyes, he saw only smoke and ash. The haze was a wash over scenes of cruel faces committing horrid acts of violence. The voices would call for vengeance and laid the weight of it at Balin's feet but he could not identify the villains. He ever sought for answers to who he himself was and why he was in such pain but heard no names. Though he screamed into the darkness, it would not reveal who was responsible. Rage was spawned that drove him in to the military to blindly seek justice for the throbbing in his soul.

It was there he found a way to make his demons tangible and destroy them. It was inevitable that he excel for he was driven to be what every general wanted in a soldier. With no other desire beyond seeking out and crushing his enemies, the ensuing years of battle earned him apprehension from many who said he was too zealous and dangerous. He was always however, the first choice when a mission called for a cold and deadly blade to slip in, execute, and vanish like a vapor.

Some say that is exactly what happened the day he deserted. After the fact, it was reported that on preceding days, he had been heard shouting and cursing loudly. Other soldiers had seen him drinking on duty but for fear of him, none dared report it.

Balin himself had become fearful for that night the voices had all synchronized and repeated a single question over and over.

"Who will make them pay?"

The words pounded in his head well beyond the sunrise like a migraine and as he felt his sanity slipping away, he began mouthing the words himself. That was the point that he took the thought as his own and for the first time saw the dark cloud over an island. He stared at the coast and the vision drew him into the interior of the country. It sailed him through dark green woods to open ground of barren white and mountain slopes. Suddenly he was soaring higher and higher above the ground and below his dangling feet he could see the outline of the entire island appear. It took him a moment or two but in time he saw it to be in the shape of a bird in flight.

He felt dizzy now and his vision blurred as the ground below began to dance. He felt sick and wished that it would stop but it moved all the more as the bird began to fly. He saw the image rise on the wind to where he floated. Soon it was coming straight at him and his heart raced like a panicked rabbit looking into the eyes of a hungry hawk. The voice he came to recognize as Rajir's filled the sky and Balin lost all feeling in his limbs.

"Behold the plagues of the Cintani! His talons have ripped life itself from you and yours. Who will make them pay?"

There was no sense in it but sensibility was far outweighed by the increasing darkness that stayed near him in the brightest noonday glare. It drove him to seek the distant lands in search of who he was and why this anger burned so hot.

With little effort and no detection he simply slipped away from his military life and never looked back. So began his roaming from one island village to another, seeking the images he had seen. He traveled nearly around the globe on tramp steamers and cargo planes with only the company of his nightmares. Card games, burglary, and occasional strong-arm robbery provided the money he needed to keep moving as he crossed the seas and searched the shorelines.

It was as Balin searched maps and local histories in a forgotten village outside Rome that he found the first pictures of the Cintani he had ever seen. He probed deeper and came across crumbling parchments ordering the extermination of a vexing sore by an elite force of shadows known only as the Tarantadei of the Darjan. They were part of a sect from somewhere far in the east and why Rome allowed them to remain was a mystery. Perhaps it was because they served Caesar that they were both feared and revered in the ancient records and looked on as mystic priests with dark powers.

The yellow scrolls vibrated in his hands and Balin felt a connection deep in his being with these men. His thoughts seemed to rile every screaming voice in his head to a frenzy pitch that spoke to him of at last knowing his destiny. Somehow he knew he could have this power and somewhere along the way he began believing that he had right to it.

With every bit of knowledge he was led to, Balin confirmed himself to be by birth or otherwise a descendant of the infamous Tarantadei. He stayed in the region for some time and gradually became one of the few living to know the story of the white tower of Cintani. He learned of the murder of his people that broke the line of the supernatural and he learned of the oath of vengeance.

The words of it were sown in his soul like a bitter herb and its strong roots wrapped around his heart and leached poison into his reasoning. He took the wicked vows of the ancients and would use all his skill to seek out this vain little bird. It had insulted the line of Darjan and robbed all the descendants. They must die so that power could be restored through the offering of their blood.

11 TALIIK

It seemed hours before the boat Balin was on reached the small cove and the hidden harbor where Balin stepped uneasily off onto the aged wood dock. His transport vessel quickly pushed back off and wasted no time chugging out of sight.

There were two old sailing vessels moored down the dock where a number of dark cloaked soldiers stood waiting. To his right on the shore he saw to his surprise, Pogis nervously puffing away at a cigarette as he paced back and forth. Balin mused at the thought of that skinny weasel screaming for help in the tunnel. He had no doubt been fetched by the two soldiers that now kept a careful eye toward him, but had no idea why they would bother. Balin now thought it a mistake to not have gone back and eliminated the liability. He was a loose end that now only reminded him and Rajir of a failure.

At Balin's inquiry, the crowd of military men parted revealing the old general sitting on a short wooden stool.

His grizzled face had been buried in a flagon of ale until he began to cough as though his lungs were about to come out.

Balin first thought him a pitiful being but as he neared, the same dread and darkness gripped his soul that surrounded Rajir and he bowed low.

"I am General Taliik," growled the old soldier when he caught his breath.

"I am second only to the great Rajir that sent you. Give me message and do it quickly."

Balin placed the message in the old hand and knew not to speak until spoken to. General Taliik grunted and slowly rose from the stool as he read the message from Rajir. He growled under his breath his displeasure at the content then coughed violently again before spitting some vile looking fluid at Balin's feet.

"These are my faithful Guard who have served me without question for centuries. I have tested each and know them all well yet I trust none completely. My sleep is little and none can tell if my eye is truly closed or not. Now Rajir has commanded that we enlist the aid of you and your misfit friend. Though I am sickened at the thought, we both know that Rajir must be obeyed."

"I have no need of that one," Balin protested but his words only irritated the general further. Taliik pointed a fat finger at Balin.

"If the Cintani God were not so cunning I would strike down the disease myself. Unfortunately, the ancient decree has given you, a descendant of the Tarantadei the right and mandate to partake in this cleansing. But make no mistake, if you are found to be unworthy of this calling or I sense your ambition to be too lofty, I will crush you and Rajir will have to find another pathetic mortal to champion his cause."

90

The general laughed and then pointed at Pogis in his amusement. "Perhaps that is your replacement there! Now go and see that you are aboard your ship. I and my company will follow."

Balin knew that in fact the old man did need him to both destroy the Cintani and please his master. He also knew that Taliik was the essence of treachery and ruthlessness and might just kill him anyway in anger. But Balin's mind seized on Taliik's mention of the threat to "ambitions". He reasoned that it might just be possible to in fact attain or even overthrow the power that oppressed him at this moment.

He hated the darkness that filled him with fear and nightmares and he dreaded every meeting with this powerful evil. But his motivations that began with zealous revenge for his people had shifted to jealous envy and lusting to break into Rajir's stronghold. For the first time he dared think it possible to reach through the spirit realms and take hold of something no man he knew of had ever had.

12 THROUGH THE WALL

An hour out to sea there was a short blast of the horn on Aldo's boat and Sophia jumped. Lucca ran to the stern and stared hard across the rolling water beyond the Christiana that followed close behind.

"It's a signal from Aldo. He's seen something.

It was a few minutes before Lucca finally spotted the first and eventually the second strange vessel that trailed them. It was not shining metal stacks and billowing, black smoke that he saw but ghostly gray sails rippling in the moonlight. They ran dark and silent and could have easily been upon them without warning had it not been for Aldo's searching eyes.

Lucca shoved the lever forward and all aboard the Casone felt her lurch forward to full throttle. Sophia watched a black puff drifting away from the Christiana as Aldo matched speed.

Those on deck murmured among themselves but Banda and his men only gazed back at the silhouettes behind them without emotion. Lucca watched the ships grow steadily closer with still some distance to Imanado. By the time the cliffs were in sight, the two faster ships had closed to within a mile.

"I hope you've got a plan Banda," Lucca said. I figure we'll barely make the cliffs before they catch us."

"It is I that now look to you! I will show you what I know but you are the true blood line and have authority in the book."

Daenos brought the one book to Banda and he held it out to Lucca.

"Open the book Lucca. It is you who must find our help within it and the passage to safety."

The dark-sailed vessels were coming even nearer and Lucca wished that he had never left harbor.

"What are you talking about Banda? There are no passages through to anywhere around here. We need to have a plan for losing those ships back there!"

"There is only one way to escape now and that is through the power of the book. Look and you will see and know. Trust it and find the words that will open the way."

Lucca reluctantly took the book from Banda and opened it to the middle. His mind raced ahead wanting to just get this over with and really do something when Banda gripped his shoulder.

"Listen to the book Lucca; it will speak the words to your heart that you must know. Listen, listen to it now."

Lucca turned the pages past the symbols that he had known so well for so long. He wished his grandfather were here. He would know where to look. He would know what this crazy man wanted.

It was that very thought that triggered something in Lucca and he began flipping pages quickly as though he knew exactly what he was looking for. Sophia watched his finger trace its way down the page and eyes light with excitement. Lucca looked up and Banda smiled knowingly.

"My grandfather loved this passage. He read it over and over to me and told me to learn and never forget."

Sophia took his hand and squeezed it. Banda nodded toward the steep cliffs and took firm hold of the helm.

"Speak them out then and we shall see if this be our deliverance or death."

"This is our plan, I talk to a rock and then we smash into it?" Lucca grabbed at the wheel and pulled against the big man's power without success.

"Do you not believe your grandfather's words to you Lucca? You are stronger than you know but you must look beyond what is there and call forth that strength!"

Balin's ships were now less than a half a mile behind. He let go the wheel as a tremor shot through him and though panic and fear sought to suffocate him something bigger began to happen.

The wind that whistled past his ears suddenly ceased and though he could see it tossing Sophia's hair all about, he could not hear it anymore. The moon drew his eye and its light increased ten times but he realized that it was not the moon at all. The moon was only a shadow in front of two eyes that shone like the sun above it. Lucca looked at the others but it seemed that no one else could see that the world had gone crazy around him. He looked back to the eyes and felt them not looking into his eyes but into his spirit. There was a burning now in his chest and his heart beat fast. He heard no words and thought no great thoughts but something had just been placed within him. The eyes eventually faded and disappeared but the heat within never did. He knew it was crazy. He knew nothing had changed but as the sound of the wind returned to his ears, he turned and faced the rock.

Lucca's voice was weak at first but with every phrase his volume and boldness grew until he nearly shouted at the high stone that lay ahead of them

"He that lays down the sea is strong and knows what lies in deep

He brings all it's creatures to serve his kin neath waves that never sleep.

His way is safe beyond the rock, though hidden in the shroud

And he that seeks with purest heart is safe beyond the cloud

I speak to stone and foaming sea and bid it to be friend

The free bird will escape the snare and jaws that seek to rend."

Break loose and carry those you love to rest on peaceful sand

Break free, break through for aid this hour comes only from your hand"

The rocks of the cliffs were only seconds away but Banda did not move his hand on the wheel.

"For Elyan and Cintani!" he shouted as the ship's bow raced toward the stone wall.

Lucca's eyes met Sophia's at the moment they should have splintered apart against the cliff but they did not. Instead, wild streaks of lightning filled the clear sky and they dove to the deck beneath terrifying crashes of thunder. Only seconds later it had ceased and when Lucca raised his head the first thing he saw again was Sophia. Her eyes and expression showed total amazement as she stared at him and then over his shoulder.

Lucca turned and his mind swirled at the sight of not solid rock but the blue green water of a peaceful river. It was not possible yet both boats chugged easily forward with its deep, gentle flow. Lucca looked up at Banda and received a smile in return.

"What just… This river… How..?"

"The river has always been here. You just never noticed it."

Lucca laughed out loud, "No, I guess I really haven't! And how would I?"

Banda unfastened his cloak and handed it to Daenos.

"Tell me, have you ever *tried* to come this way before?"

Lucca started to answer but his voice trailed off and he could only shake his head at the smiling Banda.

Banda pointed at the boat's helm.

"May I have your permission to continue at the wheel? I know the way quite well."

Lucca would later hear a similar story from a visibly shaken Aldo about a big Naarai guard named Ennui taking control of his helm and how he was sure his vessel was about to become toothpicks floating around the cliffs.

It wasn't long before everyone below deck had heard the whole story but it was quite a while before anyone was able to believe it. Everyone found place on deck and saw that they were definitely not anywhere familiar. Neither the great ships nor even the cliffs were anywhere to be seen behind them. There was only the river snaking out behind them as though they had been chugging down it forever.

The banks held occasional racks of fishing nets and small stands of fruit trees full of fruit.

"We will not need the engines anymore Lucca, for from here the waters flow homeward."

Lucca cut the motor and heard Aldo do the same. Banda brought forth a brightly colored flag and a trumpet. The flag was taken to the topmost place on the mast of the Casone and it caught the wind. Banda put the horn to his lips and blew a long loud blast as the now familiar Cintani bird fluttered along in the light breeze above them.

The sound echoed downstream and though there was no reply, Banda seemed satisfied that his message had been received. The boats drifted on as the sun dropped to the edge of the tall mountains that rose up on either side. The shadows cooled the travelers and wonder faded into weariness for most on board. But Lucca and Sophia sat on the bow to see beyond every turn. His arm was around her now without hesitation and she leaned into him and felt safe there.

13 OLD AND NEW

Darkness came and went and as the sun slipped lower in the sky on the second day, Lucca heard the sound of voices calling across the water. He sat up to search and found the source to be a dock that pushed out where the river was wide and slow.

Along the bank on either side of the moorings stood soldiers, but these were not Naarai as Banda and his men. They appeared inexperienced and few held their weapons as though they were trained to use them. All looked with suspicion at the strange craft that had floated into their world but held fast at the sight of the flag and Banda's men on board.

At Banda's signal the lines were readied and soon both boats were tied to the shore. The Naarai gathered up the weary passengers and led them off the docks and up the gentle slope of the riverbank. The other soldiers took position in front and rear as all moved toward a noisy crowd and the center of the village. Dignitaries had assembled there and the whole procession finally halted several feet in front of them.

Banda continued and all went silent as he gently pushed Lucca ahead of him and straight to the feet of a gray bearded man seated on the only chair around. Banda bowed low and Lucca did the same but sensed immediately that a line had been crossed. The captain of the village guard stepped forward with hand on sword and had the old chieftain not raised a hand, he would have drawn it. The Naarai warrior did not flinch and Lucca steadied himself with his eyes to the ground. The captain backed away still on the ready and the chieftain's expression showed his amusement at Banda's boldness.

"It has been long my old friend but as you see, my captain still holds to our traditions. Have you been gone so long that you have forgotten them yourself?"

Banda raised his head and his eyes smiled.

"Eloi, father of Cintani, I know well that none but those of your own blood may approach you unless bid. But today, I have brought you kin that you have no knowledge of. The great shakings and the sound of the trumpet you know are the beginnings of all you have believed and awaited. These are those of your own spoken of by the ancients; that were left behind. More wondrous still is their gift to you."

When Eloi stood, the old book was slowly pulled from Lucca's bag and placed in the tribal father's hands. Incredible relief came as it left Lucca's fingers and he spoke respectfully from his knee to Eloi.

"I think this belongs to you."

Eloi went pale and his own knees nearly buckled. His hands visibly trembled and his eyes grew moist as he stared. There were audible murmurings from his elders as they crowded around to see for themselves. It was some time before he regained his composure and bid Lucca to stand. The whispering in the crowd ceased as he turned to address them.

"Our village today truly does see a wondrous thing! We must now show our grace to these that have come to us. To our new friends; please accept our homes as your homes. My wife, Celeisa will show each of you a family to care for you. Eat and drink and find your rest among us!"

As the people began to greet the newcomers, Eloi turned back to Lucca and studied the battered young man's countenance. Eloi's face was now kind as the elder spoke to young stranger.

"I must ask you many things, but tonight, your wounds need tended and all must rest."

The strangers were well fed on fresh roasted fish and boiled cabbage. Water was heated in each home and everyone washed the sea-salted weariness from their skin before being shown to a warm bed of clean linens and straw.

A hot bath in Eloi's house renewed Sophia tremendously and when she was dressed Celeisa led her to her room and set the candle beside the bed. Sophia couldn't help but cry,

"I'm sorry; I am very grateful. It must be very strange for you too! It all still seems like a dream."

Celeisa sat her down on the bed and began brushing Sophia's hair. "Dreams are good things child; even when you don't understand them you should not let them go lightly."

Sophia thought back to the dreams in the cave and shivered. "It's the dreams that won't let go of me I think. Sometimes maybe I dream too much." Celeisa touched

Sophia on the shoulder and spoke without hesitation till her verse was finished.

"Listen oh Daughter

for wind, wave and stone

have whispered your name

In the voices of the water

The crackle of flame

That rides on the breeze

Say "never have you been alone"

He sounds in the deep

And he leads with his song

To a way that is sure

Though the travel is steep

To a water so pure

It refreshes the soul

And the heart will surely beat strong."

The brush was laid down and Celeisa stood to leave.

"Do not doubt your heart when it speaks to you; it will always prove true. Dream and listen with a hunger for justice and right."

Sophia lay down and the exhausted young woman was soon asleep. She did indeed dream that night and there again was the fragrance of the white flowers mixing with sights and sounds in the night. She later told Celeisa that though she never saw them, she felt the eyes of someone watching over her all through the night. She felt the same strength in them that emanated from the Naarai but even more so. Celeisa smiled and kissed her cheek.

"The eyes of Elyan have always been on you!"

14 DAYS OF WARRIORS

In the morning Lucca was amazed at how well he felt. The salve placed on his fresh bandages the night before had remarkably sped the healing of his head gash and for no apparent reason his tender ribs had become much less so. The room was full of wonderful smells and a plate of thick bacon, potatoes, and onions was waiting by the fireplace. A slice of dark brown bread and a cup of cool sweet water made this one of the best meals that Lucca could recall having in his life.

After breakfast, Lucca stepped outside and found the families that had come with him had wasted little time reconnecting with ancient relatives. Old family jewelry was shown around and someone would recognize a crest. Old names that sounded similar were found to be variations of others and even if they weren't, all were treated as the closest of kin.

It seemed that this people really had no contact with the outside world for hundreds of years and was it clear they had no desire for it either. The center of the civilization was the river that overflowed its banks every winter, flooding the low farmland. When it receded, it left behind nitrate rich sediment that fed the plants and produced abundant crops without fail. Their fruit and vegetable diet was supplemented by pork, venison and the many varieties of fish and fresh water clams available year round.

Well-tended apple and plum trees further up the side of the foothills were drooping with the heavy load of fruit and women were busy picking baskets of grapes headed for the winepress or perhaps a drying rack. Lucca saw wagons loaded with wheat coming into town from somewhere and down to the gristmill on the river. Everything was done in a slow methodical way and up till now, everything had gotten done most predictably on time.

Sophia came out of Eloi's house and Lucca saw that she had been given a clean white dress. Her hair looked freshly washed and pulled back with a beautiful ribbon. She smiled and wiped a bit of bread from Lucca's cheek.

"You look much better today; do you feel better?"

Lucca touched her hair and nodded.

"I think we're all feeling better today. This dress; this is nice! You look good in the local fashions."

Sophia pushed past the compliment and looked around her at the mountains.

"This place is amazing Lucca! These people and the way they speak; its crazy but I feel like we really are a part of this!"

"I've felt it too. I also feel that we started what ever is coming and we have to help stop it."

Aldo plodded up to them with his mouth half full of biscuit and a good size piece of cured pork in his hand.

"I don't feel much part; I can't make head or tail of

most of what they're jabberin! Food's pretty good but I don't care much for the drink; no real kick to it."

Lucca laughed and patted his old friend on the round belly that preceded him. "Well I'm glad they aren't starving you."

Aldo scowled and rolled his eyes, "Funny boy; just see if I bail out your boat again!' He ripped off another chunk of pig meat and scanned the village around them and changed the subject. "Then there's that rascal that took over my boat; he keeps following me."

Lucca looked over Aldo's shoulder and saw that they were all three under the watchful eye of the Naarai called Ennui.

"Did you ask him why?" Sophia said.

Aldo spat out a piece of gristle and shook his head. "Said he was my accompaniment or something like that. I told him I didn't want one but that didn't seem to slow him down any."

Sophia giggled. "I'd think you would like a new friend Aldo."

Before Aldo could get riled up, Lucca pointed and changed the subject. "Those soldiers over there don't look to me like much more than farmers. Don't guess they get much excitement around here."

Aldo took up the same gaze as he shaded his eyes.

"At least not till yesterday anyway."

The three looked at each other and shared a nervous little laugh. Banda was coming up the road and none knew what would happen but for now the morning sun was warm and felt good.

When the Naarai told them that Eloi was waiting, Aldo said he didn't much like meetings and was going to go check the boats. He ambled away and Lucca and Sophia followed Banda to a waiting escort of Cintani elders. The whole group then followed a grassy footpath to the long ridge trail leading high above the village. On a rock face stood a round rock building that served as a meetinghouse and in long times past an observation post

All entered quietly through the doorway then sat and waited in the wooden chairs offered them. The one book lay open on the table before them and neither Lucca nor Sophia could take their eyes away from it for very long at all.

Eloi did not acknowledge them for quite sometime. He only stared out over the river and his face suggested that he had slept little the night before

"It has been long since Banda and the Naarai have been among us," he finally said, "I am both joyful and afraid at what his return has brought. An untold time ago this book was stolen from our valley. The Old ones tell of how Conomas through greed betrayed his own people by stealing the book of ages. Men were sent after him but none could find Conomas or the book. They returned with only stories of a secret war between the Tarantadei and the The lost ones."

"The Lost ones?" Sophia said.

Eloi nodded at Sophia's question.

"Yes, that would be you! Rome rose to destroy the people of Elyan and they fought long in the towered city but were being overwhelmed in the end. When word came that Caesar meant to slaughter all, they gathered ships to flee in but there were not enough. Some chose to stay behind for the good of the many but all were sorrowful to leave them behind. They had little chance of survival for the legions were tireless in their search for us. We did not imagine that some would survive and that their descendents would return as keepers of what we thought was lost forever. Be proud, for you are children of a great people that did not give way even when all time and memory left them behind."

Eloi picked up another much worn book from the table.

"This is written of that day and remembered every harvest time."

"A sea of tears has come between
The bravest of those that choose
To give their place for love of kin
And great the treasure they would lose
To not see home or child again
To see us safe away

There is no comfort to the son
Or healing of the mother's heart
But proud are they that know a name
Of one that stayed for their own part
We sing now praise and keep their flame
In gratefulness this day."

"That same brave heart is in you, for you have had the courage to bare the one book and bring the lost ones back to us."

Lucca grinned, "I guess you could call it that. I just thought we were trying to stay alive!"

The old man continued, "Sentries were posted for years at the entrance to our land for fear that evil had captured the book and learned how to enter but no one ever returned. Not friend or enemy. We have lived in peace so long that some stopped believing the book ever existed. I myself was taught the legends but as everyone else, seldom thought I would ever see the day when I would hold it in my own hands."

Eloi turned to Lucca. "Now by bringing the ancient words of power and blessing, you have also awakened the need for it by leading ancient enemies to the mountains and our wives and children."

Sophia shook her head, "But they didn't come through. We've not seen them for a whole day now!"

Eloi's face was kind but still troubled as he recalled some of what he had been taught as a boy.

"When through the mountains and the water

Comes the blood of son and daughter

And new will come among the old

The days of warriors will unfold

The Sandosu will run with red

And every heart will fill with dread

As on its soil the dragon stands

Come through the door from other land.

There is no comfort for the young

Till ancient word through ancient tongue

Has lit the skies again with fire
Where demons hide and do conspire."

"It was easy to wait and hope for a power that never came. Now I must put all my trust in it this very hour and much of the book I do not know. They are massing at the gate and soon it will fall. The great Sandosu valley will fill with the Tarantadei and their dark Darjan. They will await us there. The battle for both our world and yours will begin. If we do not prevail and they lay hand on the book all may be lost. I fear that I fail my people for I have so little knowledge of it and so little time to study it."

"I can help you," Lucca offered, "I can help you find the answers."

Eloi turned an eye to Lucca. "Are you saying that you know the book of ages?"

Lucca nodded. "My grandfather taught the words to me before I could read myself. I know I have little understanding but perhaps together we can find what you need to protect your people. If it is true that Cintani blood empowers the protection then maybe together we can keep the gate closed. Sophia and I are descendants of this people and these, our families are also found in the pages. I had little belief but yesterday we felt its power. If you think it right, we will look together for the way."

Eloi studied Lucca's face carefully then looked to the Naarai warrior. Banda stepped forward.

"You know he is of the bloodline and I have seen his call answered when the words were spoken."

Banda turned toward Sophia. "I have seen also the eyes of hope in the soul of this woman. She too is truly a Cintani daughter and I believe that this is the appointed time. As finders of the one book, they are the sent ones spoken of in the end day cry of the poet. The gate will not stay shut. Its fall you know must follow the finding."

Banda looked at the open book on the table and leaned over it. His eyes sparkled at the sight of it but it seemed that he dared not to touch it anymore.

"Look and see that even now it is showing the way to what is to come. You must speak the words to each other now and the wisdom you need no doubt will be granted. Trust your hearts and trust each other and you will see what is right and what must be done. Now, here in this place are those that your fathers longed to see. It is a charge given to you and none other."

Eloi picked up the book and read aloud and all could feel the air become electric.

"The sword of the dragon will come one day

To the land of the Cintani bird.

When the mountain passes shall fall away.

The trumpet will sound and the shout will be heard

From the hoard that will rise against all that we love

And the earth will shake and the great towers sway.

Sandosu begins at last.

The sun will be hidden and day will be dusk

Till the battle has ceased and the rumblings have stilled

The wheat will remain on the ground in the husk

And the plowman will flee from the fields they have tilled

Then women will hide in the eyes of the mountain

But brave men stand against chance to be killed

Till Sandosu will end at last.
Their hatred is strong and through time and again
They have waited and searched for the door
The oath that has held them is stronger than men
It is cruel and has roots in the darkest of moor
And from somewhere beyond where their memories begin
It drives them to madness and thirsting for war
Sandosu has come at last.

Now come the sons and daughters through ages
With the words that bring us to light
They take to the fray where the dragon then rages
And curses are spoken and he will take flight
Then his screams will strike fear in the souls of the dead
As the truth pierces deep and his teeth cannot bite
Sandosu will end at last.
So cry for the lost and give mercy to those
Deception has buried so deep
They walk in chains of the master they chose
They are bound to destruction in vows they must keep
To a master so cruel and his passions so fierce
But the truth he denies is the pain that he knows
Sandosu will end at last."

Eloi sat beside Lucca and for the rest of the day they both spoke of the verses that were embedded into each of them. Celeisa showed Sophia paintings and tapestries brought through the wall by those who had escaped. Sophia told her what she knew of the pictures in the tunnels and that the old tower did still remain. It was late and the sun had gone when the first rumbling came from somewhere deep in the valley. It was low and steady for a moment or two then ceased. Banda rose to his feet and looked far south down the river. When it began again, it rolled like the far off sound of ocean waves beating the rocks of Totolli.

He spoke softly but all in the room felt the weight of his words.

"They will come now and the end of this age as well. But do not be afraid. It is the right time and you are the appointed people for this war. It is true also that you are not able to defeat them alone. The victory must come from Elyan and the power he has given you through the one book."

The earth shook one last time and then all was silent.

"The passage has been opened," Banda continued, "and tomorrow they will reach the valley. That is where we must meet them and face the dragon."

15 THE GATHERING OF WOLVES

Outside the cliffs, Balin cursed and struck out at anyone that came within range of his frustration.

"How could they not be here? You saw them, I saw them just a mile back and now you can't find them?'

Pogis sat nervously at the other end of the boat knowing that someone could easily be tossed overboard in Balin's rage. He was glad that it was Balin responsible to the general and not him. He was just as glad that they had lost the fishing boats too. Maybe now they would go back and he could find a way to slink away from this hate crazed lunatic. Right now, he knew that he had to stay clear of him to stay alive.

He himself had made town and gone to his hotel room to wash up and changed out of his dust-covered clothing. By the time the ferry arrived he had downed the better part of a bottle of whiskey and the horns at the dock were more of an annoyance to him than anything else. He had no thought that those he had been trailing were actually passing by within yards of him. His mind was dulled from the alcohol and his temperament was soured by the fact that Balin had almost got him killed today and then just left him there in that dark dusty hole in the ground.

He hated the big man but he feared him more. He thought that if he had the chance he would surely slip his knife neatly between Balin's ribs. He imagined it would give him pleasure to see him crumple to the floor but reality and experience told him that a man like that would not die so easily. His evil grin melted away as the more likely scenario played out with Balin stripping the blade from his hand and using it on him.

He shuddered and looked about the dark room fearing the shadows that could easily conceal the assassin. There was more than just meanness in Balin. There was something very evil that seemed to fill the air around him and he inhaled it with a great addiction. Pogis had seen him more than once mumbling prayer like phrases into the shadows and then stop as though listening. He would at times become very agitated by whatever he heard and wring his hands so violently Pogis could hear Balin's big knuckles cracking under the stress.

The air in the room would grow thick and Pogis would turn away as the fear gripped at him also. And then there were the times that he swore that there was someone there just out of vision, shifting in the shadows. Of course he never could really say he saw anyone and would blame it on the drink. But something dark had swept by the corner of his eye too many times and Balin would unexplainably know things and find people; people that didn't want to be found. That was why he knew he must find Balin first and convince him that he was not only able but anxious to aid him still. It was as he was leaving his room that night that he came face to face with these walking dead.

Without choice he found himself shanghaied and then ironically glad to see the man he hated so much. But Pogis determined that when he did leave he would not be found. He reasoned that he would have to get far away from here so he would never cross paths with Balin again. He was good at being invisible too and he would do it again, but not yet.

Now the general's ship came along side Balin's in the darkness and soon Taliik came aboard. The old man stood on deck and glared at him. Balin looked nervously about him at the cliffs and the open water.

"I don't know what happened; they were here only moments ago. There is only one small port they could have entered just beyond here. There I will find them again."

"On the contrary," the old man laughed, his voice booming over the water, "we will stay here for this is that which we have sought since the first days of conquest. The Cintani are fleeing this world and we must now pursue them and kill them but not before we discover the portal to their free land".

Taliik was amused at Balin's confusion and continued.

"We have long known that those living here were not the only survivors of the purge for there were some number that fled before the armies and escaped to the sea. But their vessels were small and not strong enough for the open water. They have passed through to a land you know not of! Your fathers searched and found no entrance but since the stirring we have heard that it would soon open again."

Balin had heard the talk and till now had ignored any notion of really finding a hidden door. His vision had been narrow and his bent on killing for the sake of killing.

"Could this really exist? It has never been seen."

The general hissed at him and Balin's eyes lowered to the deck.

"You are simple!" Taliik laughed. "The ancients foretold of this very day when we will follow this fleeing band of cowards and discover the way for ourselves! Then we will break through and destroy not just these but the whole of the Cintani race. We will take the book and their god will then serve us! This is the gate to their rabbit hole and now when all the wolves have gathered and Rajir opens the way we will pour through and devour the last of them once and forever."

As the next sun rose Balin's eyes began to make out the shapes of more old sailing vessels coming toward them. Each lowered sail and anchored close enough for him to see that they were laden with dark soldiers and all were making ready for battle. Spears and swords of every kind were glistening in the sun all around him as the open water below the cliffs of Imanado grew crowded. He had not imagined so great an army behind them in this pursuit.

Both the ships and their soldiers appeared to have sailed out of some ancient portal of time. But they did not seem to be spirits and the body armor they wore suggested they were most certainly afraid of physical harm. Balin thought back to Taliik's obvious fear of him and now guessed him to be only a man too.

Could it be that these were all ordinary men of old that walked on because of a pact with this evil? He scarcely dared to think it with the general so near but knew that this dark force to find the Cintani was using him. He also began to reason that once they had annihilated them, he would no longer be of use. On the other hand, if it were possible to overthrow the doddering old fool and prove himself to Rajir he would have both the general's place and power. The general summoned his runner and spoke boastfully loud.

"Send word to Rajir's ship that I have found the gate and that my troops are almost assembled for war. Bid him to come and force the door as the prophecies have spoken."

Taliik lifted his flagon and guzzled down a premature victory drink then wiped his face on his sleeve. He gazed to the cliffs and growled out a verse while waving his brew in front of him.

"The wall will crumble, and then give way as darkness fills the sky

The enemies will flee in fear when dragon voices cry

And all will fall and none shall rise above the dust of war

For in his tongue comes certain death and they shall be no more!"

"We will soon burst through and crush them all. The Sandosu has begun."

From a sea bird's view, the swells had now grown black with old sailing ships like so many dead flies in a pail of water. Balin watched as more and more of the Darjan arrived and spread out at the base of the Imanado cliffs. He was half sick from the constant up and down of the ship and wondered if Rajir would ever arrive. Something in him began to wish he would never see him again but it seemed that like a horrible plague, little could stop his coming.

Night fell ending the third day when Balin was summoned to Taliik's Ship. Taliik began to laugh a twisted evil laugh at sight of him and Balin hated him more than ever. Rajir's black sails had appeared in the moonlight and the last vessel to arrive had done so.

"Now you will see power revealed! Rajir will rip through this thin veil and we will bring an end to this sorry rabble!"

Taliik's eyes glazed and his taunting laugh was only halted by a violent hacking cough that finally took him to his knees. The hardened heart inside Balin was seldom moved but now it felt sick at the sight and he realized that it was pure hatred that ate away at the general's gut. He doubted there was any cure for the bitter poison the old man had drank of for so long and he knew that very liquid was pulsing through his veins now.

This was a clear picture of what was to come to him but his thirst for power like desire for strong drink had become undeniable. He had to find a way to usurp Taliik and take his place of rule. He had to make Rajir see him as a worthy replacement for the worn out and dying old fool. Then Balin would finally have the position that he deserved.

That old familiar feeling of heaviness and fear poured over him and the blackness that surrounded Rajir appeared on the deck in front of Balin and the general. They both bowed low facing the mordant cloud and dared not to move. The others on deck shrank away as the cloud grew darker and enveloped the two men. Rajir's voice rattled around them and Balin felt coldness till his bones ached.

"Are the Darjan ready Taliik?"

Taliik coughed and finally cleared his throat enough to reply as he looked at Balin and taunted

"They are ready, just as you have requested Great Rajir. I for one have not failed to do your bidding."

Though Rajir ignored the jab, Balin's blood boiled and his teeth clenched tighter.

"Then it is time to pull down the wall and loose

judgment upon those that still defy the dragon. This will be the great and final victory but you Balin, must do your part in this and gain possession of the one book. As the prophecy speaks, it must pass through your hands to me. Do not kill the bearer until I say. The transfer of authority must come from him to me through the reading of their own prophecy. I need both the book and the breathing Cintani! You must not fail in this!"

The pain was immense and Balin found it hard to speak in the acrid smoke.

"I will do this! How can we not crush them and take it with such a great force? Your Darjan will sweep them away like dust and I will give you the book!

Balin meant to speak more of himself but the air thickened and the pressure on his lungs was such that he could scarcely breathe anymore. The darkness rumbled with a ridiculing laugh that sounded more like thunder.

"I know your mind Balin! If you serve me well I will in fact reward you but if you fail me you will regret it deeply. There are things much worse than death."

When Balin thought he could bear no more, Rajir's attentions moved away and Balin collapsed on the rough wooden deck. He could see the moon again and the mocking grin on Taliik's face as he stood beside him but the cloud was gone. Rajir's ship began to move forward again without wind or oars and did not stop until it was positioned directly in front of the cliffs. There it remained without drifting and without anchor. Balin rubbed his chest and stared across the water waiting and dreading what would come next.

No man knew what happened that night on Rajir's ship but fire glowed on the bow and smoke rose high into the air. Chanting of ancient word that could not and should not be repeated drifted over the water. Pogis sat on the other ship and covered his ears in fear. Even the general sat silently listening with eyes fixed on the cliffs and the sound of Rajir's voice grew louder and increasingly zealous. Soon his voice echoed like many voices raging in an indiscernible tongue that demanded submission and waves of dread spread in every direction.

Balin could never speak of what his eyes saw that night and until much later he thought perhaps he had lapsed into a dream or hallucinations because of the strain. The whole of Rajir's ship became engulfed in flame and the fire roared and sparked skyward until it equaled the height of the cliffs themselves. From it, the shape of a huge dragon reared upward toward the sky. It roared out terrible and deafening curses as it pawed defiantly at the stars for a moment then lunged angrily at the cliffs of Imanado.

All heard the crashing and breaking. All felt the shaking. Only Balin saw the rock give way before the fiery beast reached it. Taliik screamed out in wild excitement.

"Ready on the rudder, raise the anchor and steel for war!"

The flaming wall of fire fell slowly into the sea and revealed a gaping hole in the giant rock wall. The sea now rushed forward and Balin felt their ship begin to move as they were sucked toward the opening. Rajir's ship had already entered the breach and was almost out of sight when Taliik guided their bow into the fissure.

Water continued to rush past the rocks in the gap and now a thousand dark ships were making for it. Taliik was simply giddy with bigheaded bragging as he swaggered back and forth along the bow railings. He began to laugh wildly but ended up in a violent cough that doubled him over and threatened to expel his entrails once again. Upon recovering, he looked about him defiantly and glared, especially at Balin.

"Now you see true power! If you are worthy, you will have a part in crushing these that have plagued us. I will bring the bearer of the one book before you and you will fulfill your duty to Rajir and the prophecy. It is true that it must enter your hands but know this; you must then give it to me and I will give it to Rajir whether you still breathe or not!"

Balin tried to hide his contempt for the general but his blood grew hotter and he scarcely could keep his head.

"You can be sure that I will not disappoint you and I only ask that you give me the privilege of killing this; the last bearer. This will be a day that my fathers fought and died for. Let me bring final judgment at last."

Taliik studied Balin for a moment before his scowl spread into a disturbing grin.

"You are full of hate and treachery; a quality I admire even in a mongrel such as you! It is your right as Tarantadei. It is from the sayings of old. I will grant your request if you do as I say and not cower in battle"

JIM CASH

16 VISION

The following morning, a small uproar had developed down by the docks of the Cintani village and when Lucca had heard of it he headed in that direction. When he arrived, there were several Cintani men with sour faces on one side of Ennui and Aldo on the other. Lucca was glad to see the Naarai between them but was anxious as to what Aldo had gotten himself into.

When Banda arrived and spoke briefly with Ennui, he explained that Aldo had been watching the men fish from the banks. As was his custom, he said more of what he was thinking than he should have and the men were ready to throw him in the river. He in turn was more than willing to let them try and it was only because of his new friend, Ennui that they were denied the opportunity. In a short time and a few halfhearted hand shakes it was all over and Aldo wandered back toward the village. Banda turned to Lucca and grinned.

"Your friend has no problem speaking his mind!"

Lucca rubbed his neck and kicked at a rock.

"I'll try to talk to him but he's said more than once that he feels like a duck in a hen house. He feels like he doesn't belong here."

Banda watched Aldo shuffling along with only a general direction in mind and then glare at the big Naarai guard that accompanied him. It amused Banda and his next words came out in a near laugh.

"Do you think it chance that we allowed Aldo here with you?"

Lucca thought he knew the answer.

"Why wouldn't you after all he did to help us?"

This time Banda's face laughed but his words did not come out condescending.

"Not only you my friend! His aid goes much deeper than this age and the fathering spirit within him flows from his long lineage. Though your gruff companion would deny it, his heart of mercy and thirst for justice cannot be suppressed. It has been in him and his Roman kin since the days before Menuchah and that is why his fathers helped your fathers escape!"

Lucca's heart rolled in chest and his eyes moistened.

"Does he know?"

About that time Ennui turned and Lucca saw him smile at him as though he had heard the whole conversation and Banda shook his head.

"I am sure that his heart suspects it for kindness now overwhelms him and his dilemma is in not knowing how to receive it. Ennui will stay close and be his guide on this journey. He will gently lead him to the truth and help him face the fact that he is indeed a good man."

Later when all had gathered in the stone house, Sophia sat with Celeisa and listened. They watched the men hovering over the map-covered table and she felt frustration building up inside her. It was difficult to just wait like this with such a sense of this approaching evil and she wondered what help she could be.

Sophia leaned into the warm wind coming through the rough hewed stone window and closed her eyes. There was a longing to be home, looking out her own bedroom window. She thought of her favorite beach where translucent green swells broke on the light colored sand. Sand pipers flittered along just above the surface and she remembered how much she loved the salt smell.

Then gradually, though she fought to bring it back, the white foam that washed up on the shore transformed into the small white Pamotolea. They soon covered the sand and eventually the entire scene had changed to that same flower filled meadow she had seen before. It was in fact a peaceful place and though she hadn't chosen it, the fragrant blossoms bid her to lie back and watch the fluffy clouds above. The sun was warm and as she surrendered to it, her heart began to feel light again.

But in only a moment the sky darkened and covered the surrounding mountain peeks. Suddenly, Sophia felt as caught up and out of control as the black clouds swirling wildly above her. The sun that was so warm a moment ago had forsaken her and the air took on a chill. The earth began to shake beneath her with the stamping of thousands of booted feet. There was no pleasantness here at all now but her eyes would not open and release her. As the vision unfolded around her in vivid detail, huge yellow eyes pierced what she knew was the western horizon. They were horridly repulsive eyes and she instinctively sat up and turned away from them like a bird avoiding the hypnotic stare of a serpent. It was then she saw the dark shadows and shifting shapes.

Sophia forced her eyes open and backed away from the window but the picture still remained. She could no longer be silent or keep inside her this horrible scene.

"They're hiding in the woods! I feel them in the south woods!"

Lucca and Eloi turned as she covered her mouth and waited for their rebuke. There was none and Celeisa smiled. Eloi looked to Lucca and Lucca moved to her side.

Celeisa quietly took her hand and spoke softly, "You know this?"

"Yes, I do! I mean, I don't know how but I do. I don't even know which way is south but I know they will be there." She looked back to the window and was glad to see only the gray stones again

With a nod from Celeisa Eloi asked again, "you have seen it?" Sophia hesitated but then slowly nodded. The captain called Bansani checked the map and spoke up.

"There is a grove that flanks the valley and it would hold a good many soldiers without them being seen."

Banda gave only a glance at the Naarai named Mahnuik and he slipped out and vanished like the shadow of a bird. Banda looked to Eloi.

"I will soon have word if this is true and something of their plan."

Sophia shook her head, "But I don't know what any of this means! I shouldn't have said anything!" Eloi smiled at the shaken girl.

"Celeisa was right. The eyes of Elyan are with you and you must not doubt that which you see. You must tell me now all that you have heard in your heart and the faces you have seen."

Lucca listened as Sophia gave them details of her vision that pointed him to passages in the book and specific locations on the map. Banda and Eloi verified the sites and soon a battle plan began to take shape. Celeisa asked her more about her dreams and grudgingly at first Sophia spoke of songs in the night she had always heard.

"Sing them to me child; let me hear that which Elyan has sung to you!"

Sophia's face flushed and she shook her head but Celeisa took her hand to give her courage. She closed her eyes and slowly began to hum a soft melody that no one else had ever heard. It wasn't long till Celeisa was adding a wonderful harmony that set in motion something deep inside Sophia. The sound and excitement swirled and her soul felt answers to questions she had not even known to ask. It was more than music pouring into the room and it overwhelmed all present.

Sophia heard her own voice trail away as Celeisa began to add words in the Cintani tongue. She could not understand but the more Celeisa sang the more her heart began to ache. It deepened to more than she could bear and she slumped forward in her chair and wept openly.

Lucca's soul felt it too so much that he turned away as their weight settled on him. The verses his grandfather read many times to a young boy seemed another key to the book's leading. He searched out the song in the book's pages and before long came across what he somehow knew to be it. When his fingers touched the lyric, heat flashed up his arm and straight to his heart. He looked up and Banda's countenance made him sure that the Naarai had actually seen the fire stream into him. The book vibrated under his hand and Lucca could not pull away. His mind could see the dragon of Sophia's dream and the sight enraged him. Celeisa sang on.

"The darkest came within to blind the eye from ancient truth

For lies are deep and fury rages in the mind of youth

Though pain and terror now controls the hand of brethren lost

And justice cry would be revenge when valley plain is crossed

There is but one salvation for the children gone so far

When violently they shake His soul and see of which they are

To one the revelation comes, to one the end of all

When all is lost then all is found at breaking of the wall.

They seek the words that would exalt and grant to evil heart

The highest power for foulest deeds to rend all hope apart

But it must be that right give way, redemption yearns to come

The heart that fails will sing again where all good things come from"

Lucca gazed at Sophia across the room and she felt his accolades as Eloi spoke to the whole room.

"From what this daughter has told me of her dreams, I do not doubt she shares another part of the gift given Celeisa from Elyan himself. I know now that the dragon has indeed come. Weapons will hold for a time but only by the spoken words of Elyan will victory come."

Eloi slowly circled the room and every eye was on him and the book in his hand.

"We cannot secret it away any longer. In fact, it must be held high and we must trust in its power as our fathers did so long ago. I have studied the prophecies and listened to our new young friends. My heart has surely led me to the one who will carry the one book into Sandosu for us. Celeisa too has seen the bearer of the words of power."

Lucca shook his head violently as Eloi approached him and set the book on the table.

"No, it's not me; I can't! It must be you Eloi; it must

be a true Cintani!"

Celeisa stepped toward him and he saw the confidence she had in him.

"Who is a truer Cintani than a faithful son and keeper of the one book itself? We are Cintani by birth here among the old tribes but you have also that name upon you and even more. Elyan has called your remnant back to him. You were always a Cintani and know the words of the one book better than any born here."

Lucca rubbed his head nervously and his eyes pleaded with Eloi. "I know words but not meaning. I hear something and I know it's true but how can I hold against an army?"

Eloi placed his hand on Lucca and the whole of the council rose with him to hear his final ruling,

"It is not you; it is the one book that will speak what is needed. We will protect the book bearer and trust Elyan to guide him. Already we have seen favor. I am sure right will remain strong."

The captains dispersed and the room was again awash in voices planning and assigning duties but Lucca stood dumbfounded by his new position.

Sophia leaned into his back and her arms circled his waist.

"You've already seen it work," She whispered, "and I've already seen you fight a dragon for me; what's one more?"

17 FAITH FORGOTTEN

Lucca sipped tea outside the home where he and Banda were staying. As he watched Celeisa and Sophia close the door of Eloi's house the sun disappeared behind the mountains. Darkness followed and the village soldiers were posted at every road. The watchmen's torches were lit probably for the first time anyone could remember.

"You won't be sleeping tonight; will you Banda?"

The Naarai smiled and looked at the circle of Cintani guards and the darkness beyond. "They have strong hearts and are brave men but they have not the eyes for what may enter the land they love. Their fight is coming but it is not yet."

"Why is this happening Banda; why now and who is this person in my dreams I feel so drawn to? I'm surrounded by a feeling that I've known him all my life but I have never seen such eyes before. They burn with a light that frightens me and yet I can't look away. I don't know what to make of it all but I can't wait to see him again. I know I'll see him again."

Banda looked to the west and Lucca saw him choosing his words carefully. "I cannot say as to the timing but I know I have heard the cries of pain from hearts for many years. There are cries for lost children and cries for justice from not only this people but those through the wall. Elyan is answering."

Lucca gazed across the water and back down the river.

"My family and Sophia's; some must have known that they had been left behind." Banda nodded, "All knew for a time but because they could not see or hear or touch their old lives some chose to forget them."

Lucca imagined it was much less dangerous and far less painful. Banda continued.

"Some fathers reasoned that they would spare their children the grief of the past. They explained away old traditions as simple efforts of well meaning leaders. Some grew bitter and denied that they ever were a great people. They separated themselves from the others and found it easier to avoid both persecution and the feeling of abandonment. Their grandchildren were told even less and the knowledge of Elyan and his book faded."

"How did my grandfather get the book?"

"He was of the faithful ones. His fathers held fast to Cintani ways even before the one book was carried back to them. Some even say that Elyan allowed the traitor Conomas to steal the book. The story of how he died is long but the book was regained by your kin and hid away in the caves. For centuries the Naarai have kept both it and them safely hidden."

Lucca thought about how he himself had dismissed all the writings he had heard and even memorized for his grandfather as just wonderful fairy tales. He had even intended telling them to his son someday in the same secretive manner that he had loved.

There was nothing more tantalizing to a young boy than tales of lost gold and pirates or battles with huge dragons. There was a pleasure he saw in his grandfather's eyes when he read to Lucca and even more as he mastered the old tongue and began to read the pages aloud himself. Banda stood and wrapped his cloak around himself.

"Though you did not know it, you were preparing for this day. The book is part of you and even more wondrous Lucca; you have always been part of it. There is no need to fear so sleep well tonight!"

Lucca peered deeper into the night and just for a moment caught a glimmer off long blonde hair and the quick flash of light off a Naarai sword. He considered that a fortunate sighting and the last he would see of Banda's men. It was most likely allowed for his benefit for they all moved silently and unseen yet were aware of the slightest sound or movement. That was why he was not surprised when he turned to Banda and he was gone.

18 THE BOOK REVEALED

As troops began arriving in the hills surrounding the village it became clear that this people had grown and spread robustly over the last three hundred years. It was comforting to see them marching over the horizon all afternoon but Lucca thought there should be more optimism present than was apparent. Instead he felt a growing sense of dread among the soldiers that made him uneasy too.

Captains assembled in the square were briefed as to their assignments and they in turn gave instructions to the troops they commanded. The light of campfires could be seen in every direction that night but there was very little sound. From her vantage point on the meeting house hill, Sophia could see the Naarai move among the lights until every man in every unit had seen one of the legendary warriors. She knew their mission was mostly to encourage because the people feared them yet sensed a vow to justice and would follow them when fear ran high.

Eloi had sent for Lucca and when he arrived in the stone house Banda was just finishing a debriefing of Mahnuik. As the soldier left the building Banda turned to Eloi and the council.

"We have confirmed that the woods to the south contain a great many dark soldiers and their goal is to attack our flank when we have been drawn deep into the valley."

Bansani studied the map and pointed to the ridge above the area, "There is a very narrow passage descending down through the cliffs behind them. It is not easily seen so perhaps a small number could creep down behind them and make a great deal of noise."

Lucca smiled as he grasped the idea. "If they think there is an attack behind, they may panic and come out of their cover early!" Banda's finger-painted an invisible stroke along the edge of the ridge.

"Here and here, your archers can be ready. Mahnuik will lead through the passage and if they are discovered they will be in little danger as they retreat in the narrows. In fact, they may draw a number away from the main battle and just a few men with bows above could do much harm."

All agreed and the plan was refined before orders were sent out to Mahnuik. Volunteers were easily obtained and in a short time the company slipped silently away. When all else was said Eloi and Banda pulled Lucca aside and the three of them began to speak of things to come.

A head to head battle would be the only option in the Sandosu Valley. Though it was very wide all sides were steep and there were only two ways for an army to enter.

There were actually several other approaches to the village that would afford a greater advantage to the Darjan but because of prophecy all knew that this was the ground of destiny. It had been foretold and commanded that only in the Sandosu could the book be snatched away. The landmarks had been clear and excited the dark hunters like a blood trail of a wounded animal. Eloi was more somber than ever as he spoke,

"I cannot say what will be when we reach the Sandosu. The ships that come up the river have not ceased and the Darjan continue to march into the valley."

Banda too was more serious than Lucca had seen him. "They are content to wait for sight of the one book. The Darjan knows its power but with the falling of the wall has judged that none remain that can wield it. It is to you Lucca. Look to your heart and Elyan will show us a weakness. When time comes, speak whatever the book speaks to you and it will surely be our deliverance."

The book was again placed in Lucca's hands by Eloi and the weight of it seemed incredible. It was to Lucca a great error in thinking him the worthy bearer but he alone seemed to doubt it. Celeisa touched his shoulder and when he turned she held out three multicolored feathers to him.

"You must rest and dream for I think very soon Elyan will show you his thoughts. Mark them with these for the morrow and trust in the power of the book."

Lucca had little sleep that night but dreams were plentiful; some dark and fearsome and some mysterious and fascinating. Scenes faded in and out of his head containing unfamiliar faces and places. Sometimes he would be looking up at mountain peaks and at other times it seemed the view of a soaring bird. Still, no matter where he was taken the huge eyes Sophia had described seemed a backdrop to all of it.

Sophia now sat by the fire with Celeisa and as time wore on had remembered another melody. Celeisa recalled it too and soon was singing again.

"Where unforgiving heart remain
The fellowship is missed
And what was one alas is twain
No more they offer hand of kin
But blow to brow that once was kissed
And battle as the worst of men."

Lucca felt the anger returning and hatred toward the sea of black soldier faces. It burned in his stomach like bitter wine but Celeisa's voice came drifting again and the bile of evil intent transformed into sorrow that he could not explain. He heard them taunting. He felt the hatred that ebbed from their skin like putrid sweat but her words pierced him and he could only muster pity.

"This is not Elyan's way for them
It grieves his very heart
The flame of brotherhood is dim
Dread evil toward the light is sent
But through the book and for his part
He changes all when days are spent."

Lucca felt the wetness on his cheeks when he roused from fitful sleep and searched the pages in his waking for secret words of deliverance. In the long night, feathers were placed but only two passages were chosen. There was no confirmation to him by anything but his own heart that those were right for this moment and he felt no surety of anything. He stared at the third feather and hoped something would stand out soon but it never did.

The Naarai had left them but all other leaders stayed in the meetinghouse the entire night. Food was brought but little was eaten as officers came and went till dawn. When the sky beyond the mountains filled with light, Lucca was stiff from the cold and could seek sleep no longer. It was not much longer that all left the stone house and headed for Sandosu.

Ennui had taken Aldo to the armory and found him a suitable sword and presented him with it. The old man shook his head and chuckled.

"I doubt I'll be much use to you with or without that on the field but I do know something about battles. I was in a war myself once! I don't guess you'd have heard about it around here but it was a pretty big scrap on the other side of that wall! Anyway, I seen a fair amount of fighting and I could show you a few tricks I learned along the way!"

Ennui eyed the old sailor and put forward the sword again.

"I value your wisdom friend but as you know every leader must have a symbol of authority. This sword belonged to a great man and all will know that I have deemed you a worthy bearer. Please honor me and his memory by accepting it!"

Aldo thought a moment then humbly took the weapon. "Don't seem right not to since you put it that way."

From there the two men left the village and led the old and the women with very young to a series of caves far up the mountain above the village. The "Eyes of the Mountain" as they were called, went deep and held extra food and weapons for a possible retreat. In case of a siege, there were other openings far from the main entrance that would allow escape or summoning of help.

Ennui shook his hand and left Aldo standing with the big dog at the mouth to watch the smoke rising from campfires in the Sandosu. Aldo's heart wished that he were a younger man but keeping these safe was something of worth he knew he could do. The old soldier would stay at his post and wait for news.

Eloi and the other elders assembled on a wide rock shelf behind the line of defense. The captains that would oversee the battle and send strategy from high ground were all assembled and making ready for the inevitable.

Celeisa and Sophia were also nearby with other elder wives and could see most all of the valley and the troops below. Wounded would be brought up from the rear and treated as best as possible. Sophia rubbed the knot in her stomach and watched Cintani troops move quietly past and position for the charge.

Both women of vision stared across the plain at swirls of dust that transformed into glimpses of charging soldiers and wild swinging swords. There were flashes of faces both cruel and terrified while the wind carried a thousand voices. Some were brave and full of hope while others were vicious and cold. Some were fearful yet courageous but others were driven purely by fear to some great evil. There was a blackness creeping across the plain like smoke from a toxic fire.

Sophia huddled into Celeisa's side and pulled her cloak tight around her shoulders.

"I can feel so much pain and I know we can't stop it!"

Celeisa pulled her close and stroked her hair. "You have already saved many Child! Your dreams have shown the hidden evil and your songs have both guided and strengthened even my heart! It can never be said that hope is gone because we hold the book and have seen it strong."

When Eloi summoned him, Lucca stepped forward. He had felt tension building but now as he faced these many at battle's edge, a great sense of dread suddenly rolled over him like an icy wind. It was near paralyzing and his knees would have given out but for Eloi's hand on his arm. It somehow bolstered his courage and he held the one book high.

A cheer went up immediately and rolled back and forth along the line for many had only heard that the book was with them. Sophia watched the wave of courage spread throughout the lines as the good news passed from man to man. The Naarai were nowhere to be seen but Lucca knew they had been in position most likely since the night before.

Far across the plain a low dull droning had begun. Rajir had made his presence known and the Darjan forces stopped their jostling and shoving. All faced the Cintani side of the valley and focus their attention on the coming battle through a monotone hum.

Their eyes were dull but their expressions were cruel and resolute. Cold, calloused fingers twisted impatiently around the hilt of their swords as they sank into trance like compliance to their master.

Rajir closed his yellow eyes and with the same lifeless tone muttered words of curse and evil intent in a tongue learned a thousand years ago. His chanting by some means fed instruction into his dark soldiers till in unison the pitch raised a half step. The entire west end of the valley now vibrated as every soldier absorbed the hate and anger that oozed from the black hooded form.

They felt no kinship. They felt no allegiance. They were driven only by the bond of some pact entered into in greed and held to by fear. Obey the commands of the dragon and share his spoil or take his wrath upon you.

The intensity of the Darjan chant amplified as Rajir sensed the presence of the book. Malice and loathing now dripped from every foul word he muttered as he raised a hand and pointed east. His eyes were open again and focused keenly. His thoughts had gone forth to search the bearer and a wicked grin spread over his countenance. Arrogance rose in his voice for he felt much fear and uncertainty in the hand that held the book.

There was little chance for this one to make use of it with any authority. This would be less of a battle than he should dignify but Rajir would relish crushing his foe and finally dealing punishment to the Naarai. They had long infuriated him by slashing and running from his Darjan. It was they that whisked the Cintani away to this place so long ago but there would be no running this time.

When the book was his, they would have no choice but to serve him and it was Rajir's intention to turn their swords against their own people. He would take great enjoyment in watching the pain in their faces as they were forced to slaughter the very ones they had struggled so long to save.

Taliik was standing close by and summoned Borava, his lieutenant to his side. Balin drew in close enough to hear the general's orders. Balin had been told to stay out of the way until he was needed and then he would be summoned but that would not do. If he was going to best this decaying relic of a general and take his place, he would have to show himself a superior. That would be enough to convince Rajir that he should be his general. He knew Rajir favored no one and if Balin proved himself stronger and more cunning, the job would be his.

"When the battle begins," Taliik ordered, "I want you and your best to move away from the main force and look for a weakness. Find me an edge. Look for that which they have thought most secure and capture it. Their noble efforts to protect the useless would rob them of resolve and only strengthen our forward motion. They are simple and will foolishly surrender for hope of saving themselves."

The dark soldier bowed and moved away with his men to the north side to search out the vulnerable among the thousands that now stood on the Sandosu plains. There would be no mercy shown today to the weak on either side by the dragon and the lieutenant knew that his life would be without worth if he failed. He assessed the array of the opposing side through his eyeglass and quickly picked a target area. He had no hesitation in killing the innocent and unarmed once the two lines had clashed and chaos abounded. He and his men would have little trouble skirting the main conflict before cutting through the lesser defenses at the rear and take whatever prisoners he felt most valuable.

Balin waited till Taliik became occupied with other matters before he slipped away to catch up with the lieutenant. When he found Borava, he said that Taliik had ordered him to go with the mission and identify valuable prisoners. Had not the campaign started at that moment he might have been left behind but a poor field decision on the officer's part propelled Balin into his plan.

19 WAR

"This is the day," Rajir suddenly roared, "of the dragon's power and retribution! Crush the bone and rend the flesh of everyone, for this hour I will have what is rightly mine. Let prophecy be fulfilled! Let the Sandosu come... Now!"

His voice bellowed and reverberated in the being of every soul in the valley. To the Darjan, it was the cruel voice of an exacting master. To the Cintani, it was like that of a roaring, raging dragon declaring his strength and enormous hunger for flesh. All eyes turned toward the sound and beheld the great masses of dark soldiers begin to shout and surge east. Eloi's voice was somber as he finally spoke.

"Give the signal; it is time."

Cintani lines began to advance and spread dangerously close to the tree line where the Darjan were hidden. Cintani spearmen moved along the hill below the south wood and appeared to be a sure target for those on the high ground but behind each long wide shield moved not one but two men. One carried the long shafted javelin and the other crouched, bow at the ready. They were braced for attack but would still face a dangerous dance when the unknown number descended upon them.

High on the ridge above the south woods, Mahnuik had already silently led the descent into the trees below the cliffs. His men were dressed in dark garments that very much resembled those of the Darjan in order to add to the confusion when they struck. They were few but hopefully, it would only take a small number of loud voices and several shrill trumpets to do the trick. Archers waited above and watched their progress for most of the way down. They were ready to signal at the approach of danger but the patrol reached the bottom and crept out of the small fissure without detection.

Mahnuik easily located some one hundred enemy archers and three hundred foot soldiers skulking in the darkness at the edge of the trees. Having been there for quite some time, the officers had obviously grown over confident in their level of concealment. Not a man among the dark soldiers had been stationed to observe their hind parts making it effortless for Mahnuik to spread his men out within yards of them and wait.

Taliik's instructions to the ambush was to lay in wait until nearly all had passed by then strike at the flank causing havoc with defensive positions. It was at the dragon's roar that Mahnuik gave the signal and the trumpeters blew for all they had. The combination stampeded the anxious Darjan swordsmen at the front and sent them racing down the hill in a premature start. The surprised Darjan archers had not even taken a position yet and rushed to their commanders for new orders.

With men running everywhere, Mahnuik's commandos quickly mixed among them and spread the confusion. Some urged all who would hear them to attack now by order of the dragon. Others followed the Naarai warrior as he left a trail of carnage and shouted that they themselves were under assault. The result of either ploy was hugely successful as nearly all left the trees in the only direction possible and were met with a deadly hail of Cintani arrows.

Those who chose to remain in the woods with an unknown enemy were blind with panic. They trusted no one and began fighting among themselves so fiercely that many fell before Mahnuik and the others could reach them. There are songs of the brave Cintani who fought that first battle and rightly so for no dark soldier in the wood escaped that day. It is those brave men who sing in their own verse of the terrifying swiftness in the sword of Mahnuik of the Naarai. The heroes regrouped and aided their wounded but the tall warrior only tarried a moment, then was gone.

Another scream of rage issued from the western sky as Rajir wheeled and struck his general to the ground.

"Will your mindless idiots not obey you Taliik? Perhaps you grow too old and your teeth too few to command their respect!"

Taliik struggled to rise and returned to Rajir's side like a whipped dog. "These fools have paid with their lives but I assure you Great one; they were merely diversion from a greater thrust. The battle will soon be yours and your prize will be in hand!"

Rajir growled. "It will indeed or I will position someone more capable in your stead!"

Taliik knew exactly who sought to usurp him and he turned to glare at Balin but he was not there. He concealed his alarm only because Rajir now focused his attention on the book and the bearer. Taliik's messenger was fortunate that the force of his anger only manifested now in angry words.

"Advance the archers!"

Cintani watchman relayed the enemy's movements to Eloi and the moment Lucca had dreaded arrived. Eloi nodded and Lucca opened the one book to the first passage he had been drawn to the night before. He had shown it to Eloi and Celeisa and they had both heartily agreed it would be strategic. Still he wished this place of duty belonged to someone else for every leader looked on as he stood to his feet and swallowed hard. He also wished that the third feather was not tucked in his pocket. Lucca began to read aloud the words from a book that all had put faith in but none had ever seen come to pass.

"The shaft is nock and at the call

Of trumpet sent, yet will not fall

For feathers sewn are of the wing

Of foreign bird that cannot sing

Their song of death within this land

Or bring their harm by bow in hand

So fly them all away to height

They cannot sing against the light

The arrows rise but turn their rain

Upon the wolf, upon the Bane

The terror of the sky is not,

Confusion in its stead is wrought

A thunder rolls then splits the sky,

Before the soul can blink an eye

And in its tempest blows away

The song of death sent from the grey."

When He finished, the book was closed and his eyes slowly returned to the still advancing enemy. Cintani troops raised shields in hopes of fending off the onslaught but it was a certainty that a good number of arrows would not miss. All looked for a ray of hope but in fact, dark clouds pressed in and it seemed that the dragon would turn the very sky against them.

Dread filled Lucca's heart as he watched a thousand Darjan draw back bows and aim them skyward. Seconds later they let fly into the black haze above and all could hear the whizzing sound of razor edged locusts; bent on destruction where ever they might land.

Sophia turned her back and cried out in grief against the wind for those in their path but the wind only blew her words back to her and grew stronger. It grew so strong that she had no choice except turn back around and face the horrible scene about to take place.

Her hair whipped around her as torrents of mist filled air now blasted past her heading west at greater and greater speed. When it reached the mass of uplifted shields she saw the cloud turn and through near rain all watched it push the arrows higher and higher until they were drifting back the way they came. As they began to fall, the heavy heads took lead again and soon plummeted toward new targets.

Most of the Darjan archers were restringing when they and a good number of infantry that ran ahead of them felt the sting of their own shafts sink deep. At Eloi's command, Cintani bowmen sent their own arrows west and the same wind carried them straight and long into others left standing.

As the last arrow fell, a great lightning and thunder simultaneously struck between the two converging lines and there stood the seven Naarai. Only a moment later both sides met around them clashing hand and sword in struggle for victory.

Rajir recoiled at the burst from the sky and realized his foe were not as ignorant of the book's power as he had hoped. At the sight of Banda and his warriors standing head and shoulders above all others, his anger boiled over and he leapt from his hill into the midst of his army. Taliik shouted new orders as he tried his best to follow the cloud of sulfuric black ash that trailed after Rajir's explosion forward. His own men were slammed aside like tall grass in the path of a charging tiger. His eyes were glazed and fixed on Banda who stood defiantly waiting for him.

Cintani morale now soared and they fought wildly into the advancing sea of black before them. The other six Naarai spread along the line stole courage from the dark soldiers and turned a forward offensive into defense where ever their light swords swung.

Now Banda could see the flaming blade appear in Rajir's hand and a smile spread across his face as he flew out through the enemy line to meet him. When the two swords collided, the atmosphere flexed flinging bodies in every direction for near a hundred feet. Fighting continued all around them but none dared to enter the invisible arena where Rajir swung wildly with no concern for anyone's safety. Banda met each blow with equal strength but neither clearly took the upper hand in this supernatural combat and Rajir let go a treacherous laugh,

"Long I have dreamed of your fate Naarai and today you can run no more! I will be your king and ruin!"

Taliik's lieutenant Borava and his men had by this time made great progress. By murder and theft they had taken enemy cloaks and secreted themselves and Balin all the way to the tents at the rear of Cintani lines. Balin peered out through a slit in the canvas at the goings on and pointed.

"There is your goal Borava; secure those and bring them here to me."

The lieutenant assessed the risks for a time and determined his unit's skills to be ample to take on this mission. Balin waited only a moment after they left to slip out the other end of the tent and move toward his goal; power.

20 THE THIRD FEATHER

The council on the rock vista was not speaking openly but it was apparent that all were jubilant at the appearance of the Naarai. Not only had they stopped the Darjan advance but it seemed that they were slowly starting to push them back. Lucca was amazed and more than anything else relieved when the Naarai appeared. His faith in the book rose to a new level and his confidence to speak now grew also. That is, at least until Eloi spoke again.

"What now will you speak Lucca? What would Elyan give the bearer to declare over us and his enemies?"

Lucca opened the book to the second feather marker and studied the lines. He had been fairly sure the night before but here in the heat of the fray, his mind had doubts about his second choice. The third choice was now even more of a mystery to him.

"This doesn't seem right Eloi. I thought it was last night but now it just doesn't seem to fit with where we are!"

It made so little sense to him and he thought perhaps that he had confused the order or page. There was nothing there however, on either side that felt as right to his heart as these words.

"We do not see," Eloi encouraged, "the whole of Elyan's heart, but you may be sure that all in his book is good and no word treads outside of his purpose. I have placed my trust in you for no small reason."

Lucca weighed Eloi's word against this feeling a moment longer but finally trusted the something or someone, that this was the page. He stood again and those who were skeptics before listened and anticipated as much as any.

"For love of fair one

He will give

The words of life

To death, to live

Against all hope

We see it lain

For truth is scarce

And trust is slain.

The heart is torn

To do the right

For good of all

Or save the slight

But this we deem

Act of a fool

Will not give evil

Right to rule

The sacrifice

Is not the end

His truth of truth

Does not depend

On mortal men

To see it through

The greater love

We see him do."

"Darjan are in our midst! They have Celeisa!"

All were caught off guard by the screams that interrupted Lucca's reading and drew their eyes to the black knights holding several women including Sophia and Celeisa. The alarm had come as a surprise to Borava also for he had taken extra care not to be seen. He had no choice but to put backs to a stonewall and knives to the hearts of the hostages.

"Stand away unless you wish them dead and their blood on your hands! I will not be bothered in the least if I leave them all without breath!"

Every extra man with a sword had rushed to surround them but now held back at the threat. Lucca broke through to the front only to see the terror in Sophia's eyes and the ruthlessness in Borava's.

The moment mayhem broke loose, Balin smirked and

stepped among the crowd. It was he who shouted the first warning and betrayed Borava's position for this very purpose. With all the others, he rushed unnoticed toward the scene and in due course caught sight of Lucca. The big man did not slow his pace as he neared but instead, lowered his head and rammed the book bearer squarely between the shoulders at full speed. Lucca's head snapped back in the violent motion that flung him tumbling into the midst of the Darjan standoff as well.

Balin's blade was quickly against Lucca's neck and suddenly the course of the entire war was at stake. When Borava realized who and what was at his feet, he and his men encircled Balin and Lucca holding the women out as shields. Lucca clutched the book and hoped that his attacker had randomly taken him hostage with no knowledge of it but hope promptly fell away.

"He will speak no more if I open his throat," Balin laughed, "Stand away for your cause is lost!"

Lucca felt the knife edge just below his chin as Balin dragged him to his feet and put a steely grip on the back of his neck. He offered no resistance for he could see Sophia's arm twisted cruelly behind her back and the Darjan sword's intent. Eloi watched his own Celeisa struggle against the painful constriction of her arm and motioned the Cintani guards back.

As a way opened, Borava and his men slowly moved with their circle of prisoners back toward the front lines. The stunned defense forces parted as Eloi walked ahead to insure them safe passage through. The sound of the sobbing women at his back put ache in his heart and tears blurred his eyes. Lucca's last reading reverberated in his mind and a clearer understanding of what he must do as a leader and not a husband pierced his soul.

"…The heart is torn
To do the right
For good of all
Or save the slight…"

His choices left little chance to save his beloved and in overwhelming Borava to regain the book, Lucca would most likely be lost as well. With Elyan's words, he could give his people another chance against the dragon but all else that he loved and lived for would be lost.

"Don't give up Sophia; don't give up!"

Lucca's words felt hollow and he realized that they might have been more for his benefit than for her. Sophia's neck twisted and in the second that their frightened eyes met, it seemed that a lifetime of unsaid words were spoken and every unimportant offense forgiven. Balin laughed and squeezed at Lucca's neck harder but it only revived a will to find a way out of this.

The front lines were in sight now and as the rows of Cintani soldiers parted, the Darjan forces recognized Borava and ceased their attack. The intense battle of a moment before quickly became an uneasy standoff with no one knowing quite what to do next. Eloi knew that in a few more steps, all would be lost. With thousands of Darjan just yards in front of him it was perhaps already too late when he turned and stood blocking Balin's way.

"You hazard the life of your champion old man! Step away or I will bleed him here and now!"

Balin's arrogant shout did not shake Eloi as he looked into the eyes of Celeisa and replied evenly.

"You know you cannot; your master must have this heir for his purpose. If you slay him, there will be no voice to abdicate power to him. You know the dragon is far too greedy to simply destroy my people. Deny him the allegiance of our god and it will not go well with you when he learns of it."

There was a silence for a time before Eloi heard the unexpected reply. "You have misjudged as to who will be master and who will serve!'

Lucca was suddenly thrown to the ground and Balin's big boot came down heavy on his chest. The book was wrenched away from him and troops on both sides recoiled as a shock wave of power shift blasted across the valley. Balin addressed the lieutenant as he sneered at Eloi.

"Stand with me Borava; you will be my General and Taliik will serve at your feet!"

There was little hesitation before Borava made another poor choice and ordered his men to stand firm around Balin.

Eloi watched in disbelief as the wild-eyed Balin's filthy black fingers cracked open the pages and looked inside. When the book was opened, Borava sensed something that made he and his men hold tighter to their hostages but move away from Balin and his ravings.

It fell open to the center and to Balin's delight he saw a picture of the dragon standing in the midst of battle just as Rajir's prophecy had said there would be. This was Balin's chance and no longer would he cower in fear to Rajir. He would keep the one book and not only rule over the Cintani God but all the forces of Darjan as well. That included making Rajir pay for his years of torturing him.

Where Lucca lay on the ground, the horror of the moment clutched at his throat. It seemed all was lost and he had failed his people when they needed him most. Balin himself could scarcely believe he had at last put his hands on the one thing that had eluded him for so long and he let out a screaming yell of triumph.

Banda somehow heard that howl across the valley and in a splintered second, vanished from under the swing of Rajir's flaming sword. With nothing to strike, the weight of Rajir's blade carried him around in a half circle and sight of the place Balin stood. His repulsive form glowed red as he sensed the there had been a blow against the Cintani. He looked again for the Naarai before turning his attention in the form of a full run, back to the book.

Balin saw cruelty itself coming as stunned soldiers in Rajir's path were trampled or knocked out of the way. He dragged Lucca back to his feet and shoved the book in his face and there was desperation in Balin's voice. With faces inches apart, Balin whispered with rancid breath,

"You will read this Cintani! You will speak the words that declare me the victorious dragon!" Balin grew angrier and intensified his threats as Lucca hesitated. There was little time now for Rajir's outline on the southern horizon was ever growing larger.

"Take care if you think to deceive for I now have the power to know your mind! If you refuse, I kill all of these and also destroy your precious book!

It seemed a chance glance that brought Lucca sight of Eloi where he stood just beyond Borava's circle of men and there was no question in Lucca's mind now that Balin had to be stopped. He knew fully what that meant to him and he steeled himself to hear Eloi's order to attack. He did in fact see Eloi's lips moving and recognized instantly the words silently being formed.

"… *But this we deem*

Act of a fool

Will not give evil

Right to rule…"

Lucca remembered the words Eloi had spoken only a short time ago and mouthed them under his breath. "All in his book is good and none of His words tread outside of his purpose."

It was then that the last feather fluttered from his hand.

Balin struck Lucca hard in the face and cursed,

"Speak it!"

He now knew what the third passage was meant to be and without another thought, Lucca quietly began the passage that Balin's big finger demanded.

Balin Shook Lucca.

"Louder! Speak it louder!"

21 THE POWER COMES

Eloi raised a hand as Lucca raised his cracking voice and all went silent to hear the words he shouted.

"The Fathers fall before the hoard
And dragon reaches for reward
The sun now strikes the broken sword
And all will feel the blow

The earth doth shake as fire falls
And blazes round the one who calls
And from the ancient palace halls
The power now must flow

Oh bring the vision full of sight
Within the brilliance of its light

That strips away the will to fight
And courage flees away

The spoken word from ages past
With untamed power fully cast
On this consuming lust at last
Pours out upon this day"

Lucca stopped reading but continued to stare at the page. There was only the wind above Balin's heavy breathing and he had paid little attention to Lucca or the words but instead watched Rajir continue to move toward him. At the realization that nothing had happened, his eyes shifted from Rajir to Lucca, then the words under the dragon's picture.

"Again; you must say them again or I will…"

The threat was cut short by a rush of wind and the sky was pierced by a sword of blinding light centered on Balin, Lucca, and the book. The ground shook and everyone close including the mighty Rajir, stumbled and fell back. Though he growled and snarled in his anger, he could not move forward or even look at the brilliance.

Sophia screamed as the Darjan guard fell on top of her. Celeisa closed her eyes and covered them with her free hand. Eloi tumbled backward but never turned away and he strained his eyes to see beyond the veil of light but could not.

But in that light, Lucca and Balin both saw the picture of the dragon come alive on the pages before them. It moved with an army around it slashing and burning and enslaving all before it. Then it took children from dead mothers and in disgust they watched it make them suckle from a breast that appeared from under the scales.

Time accelerated and the children grew and served the dragon and hated their own people. They joined the ranks of the army and pushed across the land stealing other babies and brought them to the dragon for it could not reproduce on its own. But even those she raised she hated and eventually destroyed for they reminded her of her bareness.

The vision pulled in close as another helpless child was brought toward the beast in the arms of what was now clearly a Darjan soldier. Both men could now see into the eyes of the tiny baby and both somehow knew without a doubt the child's name.

When the light and pictures faded, all could see again but Rajir was first to rise and slowly approach. Borava and his men had dove to the ground but quickly regained control of their hostages and waited to see whom they would now serve. Rajir cautiously began to speak with snake like cunning.

"Give me the book Balin! You know you are not strong enough to wield it but I can and will grant you all the power you desire! Give it to me!"

Balin turned. It took a moment for his eyes to readjust to the dismal light and see the dark face of Rajir with his outstretched hand. The next thing Balin noticed was the absence of fear even though he knew Rajir meant to kill him as soon as he had the book. There was no longer that strangling oppression on him in the presence of this evil.

"I will give you what you desire Rajir. I will give you the words of the one book."

Balin stepped toward Rajir but kept the book close to

his chest until they were inches apart. Rajir again put forth his hand; eyes fixed on the prize and Balin took his chance. His left hand came up quickly and drove the long blade of his knife neatly between the chinks of Rajir's armored breast plate. Rajir gasped and his eyes showed the shock as the blade was twisted and pushed deeper.

"I have believed a lie," Balin whispered, "Because my fathers believed it, I have murdered my brothers and all but destroyed that which is the only real truth. You will not have this book and the dragon will die here and now!"

Balin pushed again on the knife but Rajir's expression turned from surprise to anger. His right hand seized the book and his left landed a powerful blow to the side of Balin's head that sent him sprawling. Balin hit the ground hard and in his dazed condition saw Rajir holding the book and pulling the knife from his chest. There was no more than annoyed disgust on his face as he inspected his wound and threw the bloody blade carelessly away.

"Stupid man! I cannot be defeated by the likes of you who thought yourself equal with me! There are thousands of fools like you that will do my bidding. Now that I have the one book you are useless, but to kill you is below me. I will send another to do such an insignificant task."

Balin could hear the rasping laugh of Taliik but lost consciousness as Rajir's attention now turned upon Lucca. An unseen power jerked Lucca off the ground and brought him face to face with the most evil he had ever felt in his life. There were only those wicked yellow eyes to see beneath the jagged edges of the hooded form but the wicked voice rang harsh in his bleeding ears.

"And you; you see now that no noble action can spare your race; save allegiance to me. Now save yourself and these, your pathetic friends. Speak forth the words again that open up the sky. Then you will see this glory bestowed upon a worthy ruler. Quote the prophet and give me that which I deserve."

Lucca's heart was to defy Rajir and die. He would have to find another Cintani to read the words and that would give Eloi a way to stop this nightmare.

He was about to refuse when time and light somehow flickered and the Naarai were instantly there around those holding Sophia and Celeisa. Borava braced for attack but Banda's men held still and silent without even drawing sword. Their fiery eyes were all trained on the one book and its new possessor. Rajir laughed as he opened the book again to the strategic page and lifted it to Lucca.

"You are too late, warrior! No matter if you strike my whole army down; he is mine! Soon, every sword including yours will be mine as well! Your very purpose has ended!"

Banda replied without angst.

"You will do as you wish Rajir; of that I am sure. See now if Elyan's power is what you really desire."

Banda gave nod to the battered Lucca and did not back down in the least. Lucca's heart was numb now but at Banda's prompting, spoke the words without emotion. Rajir's pleasure was on his face and when the passage was read, began to laugh his darkest, mocking laugh. Lucca was tossed aside like a rag doll and the earth shook again. Rajir stood holding the book over his head like a trophy and still the Naarai did not move.

"Now Elyan," he roared, "I hold your precious book! I command you! You must tell it to obey me now! Send its power upon me!"

All watched the blinding light come down for the second time around Rajir. All saw him spread his arms to receive it but only Lucca saw in Rajir's being that something was very wrong.

What happened to Rajir, not even Lucca saw for the

light and power intensified so much more this time that he disappeared within it. A deafening dragon's roar of victory that had filled the valley suddenly twisted into horrified scream. In the same instant, Naarai swords flashed at the edge of the blazing light and all those holding the women captive crumpled headless to the ground. Sophia felt for Celeisa's hand and they crawled with eyes tightly shut, away from the dreadful sounds behind them.

The column of light had hit the ground and spread like an inverted mushroom cloud to every end of the valley. All in its path fell to knee and those who were wise fell to their face under the power of this weighty presence. The sound of thunder rang in every Cintani ear but Darjan soldiers heard the rumbling as words clear and terrible.

"Listen, you of the Darjan; I am calling to you as sons I have lost! This is the day of decision and if you dare look, you will see truth in this light. Deceit of the dragon has robbed you of your rightful place in my family but I offer you rest among these people. Forsake the hatred that has no regard for you for there will be no contest when I loose the sword of the Naarai. It is still for you to choose. The dragon held you with lies and threats. I will not."

Immense fear came over the dark soldiers and a great many did lay down their weapons. The defiant General Taliik and those with him who would not lower their swords watched them crystallize and turn to powder in their hands. Some say their hearts just stopped within them and they fell dead. Others say they had no hearts and the evil that sustained them was finally driven away. The shells that once held mortal men simply collapsed. In every account however, only those that humbled themselves remained alive a moment later.

Only Eloi was shown in that split second flash the speed and precision of the Naarai blades but it was so terrible that he never spoke of it to anyone. "Soldiers of

Light", he called them from that day forward.

Lucca feared going blind but he could not turn away. There in the white light were those most incredible eyes again. They moved toward him and the shape of a man formed around them but only that much. There was no mouth but the eyes were smiling warmly and inconceivable joy flowed out. Lucca felt himself smiling and even wanting to laugh. Had he gone mad or was it really possible to have this much peace when all had gone so wrong?

He closed his eyes and still the figure was before him so he reasoned that this must be what it was like to die. He was amazed at how much it was like life and he wondered when all these aches and pains would go away. He thought perhaps it was coming in waves but he wondered how much more of this elation he could stand.

Little by little Lucca was no longer looking at the eyes but through them. He was now standing in the light and there before him was a wounded and weeping Balin. His form was translucent and Lucca could see a battered heart just barely beating. He now understood that this was a lost brother. Hatred had been born in horrible deception and passed down through generations to this stolen child. Compassion came from deep inside of Lucca that left no doubt of his obligation.

He realized he was not dead and his thoughts went again to the book but though he searched all around him, it was gone. His heart sank for through these eyes he could not turn away from Balin and the many others that lay wounded. There was a great need now and he had lost the only hope this people had to cling to. That was when he felt the light saturate his soul and every cell in him heard what he never doubted to be the voice of Elyan himself.

"This people have forgotten me and only served my book, but I have come now to be life to all who would know me. You must not forget the books of old but know that life is not in them. I have placed it in you. You are my testament to all and I write on you my will and desire.

Lucca hung his head, for still he felt that this could not possibly be something he could carry. But the fire inside him only intensified and the message grew stronger.

"It was never the book that held the power. It is my people that carry my authority over death and sickness. My words within you are the sword of Elyan that was always meant to heal. When put on the lips of the hungry, they summoned the good harvest. But it was not the book but I that revealed the hearts of men to you. It is not the book but you that are my most precious possession. I am pleased that you have put it above your own life and have resisted the evil ones. But now, if you speak words of forgiveness, you will heal them all."

The soft touch of Sophia's fingers on his shoulder brought the world around Lucca back into focus and he embraced her for the longest time. Balin was stirring and Banda stood over him with sword still drawn but it was not to slay him. Lucca understood that Banda saw the change in Balin and was there to protect him from angry Cintani swords. The eyes within Lucca could still see the pain and despair contained by the man. He began to weep for him and could not restrain from reaching out to the one who had moments ago sought to murder him. The broken Balin was drenched in shame and drew back but Lucca's tears confused his fear and calmed his mistrust. Lucca realized that he had not finished the verse he had begun and now as he did so, the words washed over Balin like cool water. The big man went limp and tears that had been pent up far too long were released by the sound of Lucca's voice.

"For what is more

To slay and end

The life of one
That once was friend?
Or heal the wound
And bind the heart
I choose forgiveness
For my part."

22 A NEW CHAPTER

In the months following the war, envoys from both sides met in the meeting house and those of Rajir's army that survived, heard and accepted all terms of surrender. A proclamation of repentance was issued and read in every Cintani province stating that,

"Our deception under the dragon was great and our transgressions grievous. No demon or anyone who serves a demon is content with their station in life. They are filled with festering sores of envy and jealousy. For the very nature of the one they serve is to ascend beyond his place and become God by theft, destruction and murder and it is written that they will become like those they serve. It is only to gain power that they submit and then only until they are strong enough to over throw and seize the authority of another. Hatred and greed drive them and only fear holds them back. There can never be joy or peace in such an alliance; only certain death. We seek the mercy and forgiveness of both Elyan and the people of this land."

It took some time before anyone was able to understand but with Banda's help, Lucca and Eloi spoke of the new alliance to every Cintani man, woman, and child. It took just as long to assure the surrendered dark soldiers that they were truly free from Rajir. Eloi declared a new name over them. He called them "Akouo" which means, "Those who have heard," and told them that there was room in the land of the river for all if they chose. They heard and were grateful, but most feared the Cintani and left the valley to lands far in the south.

There was as much doubt among the Cintani that so many would so easily forsake their murderous ways to live in peace. Those who had lost loved ones in the war were the hardest of heart and criticized those that welcomed the dark soldiers to the light. They sought punishment instead and would have most likely started a new war had it not been for fear of the Naarai that stood with Eloi. Eloi did his best to bring all sides together but there would be divisions and hurt separating old friends and families forever.

Balin's associate Pogis had been missing since the battle but no one had seen him among the living or the dead. After several months however, Daenos approached Balin with news that a man matching his description had shown up in a small farming community in the northern hills. He offered to take him there and soon they had climbed to a high mountain village where crops were grown on the sunny terraced hillsides.

To Balin's surprise, they found the once devious little man tilling soil with honest sweat on his brow. Apparently, he had crept away from the Darjan ships during the fighting and sought to hide among these farmers. In time he found that he had both a fondness and a gift for growing and decided to stay.

He nearly fainted at the sight of Balin and had they not offered him water and shade he might have indeed done so. A second dizziness took him when Balin asked forgiveness and told him of his own change of heart. They learned that he had taken the name Anothen which Daenos said suited him more than his old one and that he should keep it. It only seemed right to let him stay there if he wished and he did, so they shook hands and parted as friends. Daenos would stop by every few months and Anothen eventually believed that he was not there to kill him. He did not however, get use to turning around and seeing the fearsome soldier suddenly standing there.

No one could deny that Balin was indeed a different man too since the light had touched him. Lucca began to teach him about his real heritage and he would listen many times to the stories with tears on his face. There was deep sadness in him at these times as he confided in his new friends.

"Since his eyes have fallen upon me I have done little but regret my sins, but Celeisa is helping me see Elyan's kindness also. I only hope I can live in gratefulness to his mercy."

Eloi and the leaders all saw his sorrow for his past but they were among the few that would speak kind words to him. Even as Balin tried his best to make restitution, only some were able to forgive him and none could forget that day in the Sandosu valley. As months went by he told Lucca that he thought it best if he too left the river land for the good of all.

Lucca was against it but it was Aldo who helped him see that not only was it hard for Balin here but also dangerous. Eloi and Celeisa counseled with them and it was agreed that Balin would be free to leave. When they approached Banda as to where he might go, Banda consented to escort him either deeper in to Elyan's land or back to the land beyond the wall.

"There is no land," warned Banda, "where the past will not haunt you my friend but you can be sure that where ever you tread, Elyan sees and will send you comfort if you call."

Eloi, Celeisa, Lucca, and Sophia were all there at supper the night Balin said his goodbyes and left with Banda to the other side of the wall. He would go quietly so none would follow but showed his sorrow now at leaving his only friends.

"Let all that seek my life know that they have no more to fear from me in their land and though I will miss you all, I will not speak of you or seek to return for their sakes. I do ask one thing of you and that is that I may return to the caves beyond the tower and restore honor to the room of history. Since I have met the truth and know the sound of his voice, my heart thirsts to know more of him. It would be some atonement to make them safe."

Banda put on his long gray cloak and Balin felt him look deep in his eyes as he spoke.

"There was a man who lived his life along the edge of shadows and light and everyday he arose hoping to just survive the endless toil of simply existing. And then one day he found himself in the presence of a king who told him that he was his child.

"But how could this be," he cried, "for I have watched you from afar oh King and never dared to draw near to your powerful majesty?"

"Ah," said the king, "it is I who have watched for years and longed for you. I have always loved and called to you!"

"That voice!" the man whispered, "that small voice I've heard since my mother's womb! It was you! I thought myself insane for it called but I knew not from where!"

Then the man bowed his head and wept as he knelt before the king.

"My treachery has carried me far from you and I have branded myself an enemy of the crown. Now I am apprehended and you do justly and well to strike me down for my crimes are many!"

Sorrow and regret held him as he waited for the sword. He felt only hot tears upon his head and shoulders and through his weeping, the king spoke.

"My son, I have suffered for you and it was enough. Now you must come full into the light and see I have given you covenant and power to drive back the darkness. Most of all, you must live in my house and eat and drink with me. Nothing would please me more than your acceptance of my love. You will not hold it all in a single lifetime, but I have made remedy for that also."

Balin's face was wet as Lucca and Sophia embraced him. Eloi gave him a leather necklace that held a small silver bird in flight. Celeisa kissed his forehead and whispered in his ear.

"You will be written of as a true son and a worthy keeper of our history in the old world. As the new Cintani book will now be written, you were born new and your pages are clean in Elyan's sight. I know he will fill them with words of compassion and faithfulness."

All watched the Banda and Balin slip away down the riverbank and Lucca wondered if he himself would ever return to the sea beneath the cliffs of Imanado. There was still much to be done here to assure lasting peace and the other families showed no sign of wanting to leave. The war had brought those from both sides of the wall close to their newfound kin and all seemed quite content. It was perhaps a redeeming of heritage lost and a way to regain some of what fear of the dragon had stolen.

Eloi had felt the question coming long before Lucca asked it. "Can the river ever be open to all or would more darkness come looking for Elyan's book?"

The elder tried to smile but his eyes gave away the heaviness of his heart.

"We must teach that we are all the bearers of his words now and every vessel is blessed and powerful. When all know who they are, they will leave fear behind and desire will change the river's course. Then His words will flow back to the sea and other lands will again hear his call as well. There is hope always when those who believe in Elyan's goodness do not falter."

Sophia began to sing softly and Balin and Banda were almost out of sight.

"Journey far my friend

And take for your cloak

Garments warmed in

Elyan's fire

They will keep you from

Weary rains that soak

And will shed all

Evil's dark mire

You will find your way

To a harbor sure

You will find your voice

In his word

Healing comes from you

With a heart so pure

Like the song of

Cintani bird. "

"He is not without hope and they will not be without light," Celeisa comforted, "Elyan goes with them even now and someday I think you will follow. The new book is begun.

End.

CINTANI WORDS

Cintani: (Sin tah nee)
The Ancient Race that Rome sought to wipe out because they would not bow to Caesar.

Menuchah: (Meh-noo-chah)
The Cintanian city destroyed by Rome
Its name means a resting place: waters of quietness.
Caesar hated the name.

Lucca : (Loo-cah)
The handsome young fisherman

Sophia:(So-fee-ah)
The Pretty young Island village girl

Aldo: (All-doe)
Lucca's cranky but good friend and fellow fisherman

Yakolai: (Yah-ko-lie)
The name of the island where Lucca and Sophia lived
The Hebrew root Yakol (yä ·kole) means to overcome.

Kerdainō: (ker-dī ·-nō)
Lucca and Sophia's village on Yakolai
Hebrew root means:
To win
To gain Christ's favor and fellowship
To win anyone over to Christ
Escaping evil
To spare oneself

Totolli:(Toe-tall-lee)
The northern most tip of the island where the waters are shallow and exposed to the open sea winds. The

shallowness of the water and the wind make it unsuitable for boats and living. There are a few abandoned shacks there but no people.

Imanado: (M-in-ah-doe)
Large cliffs overlooking the sea at nearly (but not quite) the south end of the island.
Above the cliffs are layers of rich soil and flat farmland where most of the crops on the island are grown. No one lives there but many live on the road to the north that stretches between the highland and Kerdainō through the Copani valley.

Votadi: (Vo-tah-dee)
A small island directly west of the tower about ten to fifteen miles.

Copani: (Ko-pah-nee)
Copani was a small green valley on the back side (Northwest) of the Imanado farmlands where waters congregate and trickle down the mossy rock walls for a considerable distance before finally forming a small stream that then turns northeast. It then runs down and around the back side of Kerdainō and then to the sea under the north bridge .There is a road from the southwest end of town that leads to the valley on it's way to the Imanado highlands. The south bridge crosses the stream again a short distance from the source. Many of the farmers stop there to rest and water their animals.

Taba Trees;(Tah-buh)
A short and unattractive form of a locust tree brought to the island as seeds mixed in with animal feed. They spread quickly and are hard to kill out even in dry ground.

Pamotolea: (Pah-moe-toe-lee-ah) The name means: "Cry for justice"
Small white flowers with five petals and thick powdery white leaves that bunch around the clusters of blossoms and keep them from ever touching the dirt below. The pudgy tear shaped leaves on close inspection have just a tinge of green in them but it would never be seen from even a short distance. In fact, the entire plant blends in with the dry white ground where Sophia first saw them. Many people pass them by and never notice the hidden beauty beneath their feet. The interesting thing is that they appear in both extremely dry and very wet areas, sometimes covering entire fields. Even more strange is that when water is plentiful, the leaves turn bright green and the petals produce a wonderful fragrance.

Tarantadei: (Tah-ron-tah-day)
Assassins sent by Rome to infiltrate the remaining citizens of Menuchah. They vowed to find and kill all the missing Cintani. They were part of a dark eastern cult called Darjan that Caesar himself probably feared. His decree to let them remain in Rome was never understood by even those in his own council because the Darjan were never required as all others to pay tribute. Some writings even suggested that failure to compensate Darjan fairly for the use of the Tarantadei was directly linked to Caesar's death. In any case, it was an evil partnering to be sure.

Sandosu: (San-doe-soo)
The valley of the great battle.

Balin: (Bay-lin)
The Assassin

Pogis: (Po-giss)
The reluctant but greedy assistant to Balin.
A petty thief and informant by trade that happened one night to be recruited by Balin to find people or old stories for money.

Eloi: (E-low-eye)
Leader of the Cintani

Celeisa: (Sell-ee-sah)
Eloi's wife

Bansani: (Bawn-zah-nee)
A military man under Eloi

Naarai: (Nah-ah-rah-ee)
The mysterious soldiers

Banda:(Band-ah)
Leader of the Naarai

Orani: (Or-rah-nee)
Orani was a small fishing village on the opposite side of the island from Lucca and Sophia's home. The mainland ferry would run first to here, then down around the cliffs of Imanado to the south, around the point and up to Kerdainō. From there it would return to Orani and then back to the mainland. There was little north of Orani worth seeing. There was one small cove northward but it was open to the rough sea in the winter and the black shifting sands were always changing the bottom of the inlet. A boat of any size could easily be foundered and risk of capsizing in the high waves was great.

Casone: (Kah-zo-nay)
The Name of Lucca's fishing boat.

Cristiana: (Kris-tee-ann-ah)
Aldo's boat

Polani: (Poe-lawn-ee)The busy body Mrs. Polani

Leviathan: (Lah-vie-ah-thun)
Aldo's dog

Daenos: (Day-nohs)
Second in command of the Naarai.

Rajir: (Rah-jeer)
The dark presence and leader of the Darjan army
General Taliik: (Tah-leek)
Subordinate to Rajir

Ennui: (In-you-I)
Another of the Naarai

Mahnuik: (Mah-new-ick)
Another of the Naarai that led the ambush

Borava: (Bore-rah-vah)
An underling of Taliik's command

Tatiana: (Tah-tee-ah-nah
Lucca's mother

Ludwena: (Lood-wee-nah)
Tatiana's sister and Lucca's aunt

Yauvot: (Yah-vote)
Lucca's Uncle

Thaliana: (Thall-ee-ah-nah)
Sophia's mother

Marcos: (Mark-ohs)
Tatiana's brother and Lucca's other uncle.

Sotro: (Soh-troh)
A city on the mainland that Pogis lived in.

POEMS AND SONGS
OF THE CINTANI

"The Way out"

"Fly away with tiny wings
Make your way to light
His hand is there
To loose the door
And keep you safe
In fear's dark flight."

"The Dragon"

"The people lived in fear,
For there was no one there
Strong enough to fight the dragon
And end his reign of death.

The old ones told of one
Who came so very long ago
And took away the dragon's power,
But how could that be so?
For the dragon still could plunder
And make our hearts grow weak,
Then another of the old ones slowly stood to speak.

The power of the dragon
Is not power of his own,
The power belonged to someone else,
Though very few have known.
"Then who" we cried,
Has given back the dragon of their might?
If he has given, he must take it back!
He must fight!"

"The Lines Lucca Left Out"

"The power was your own He said
But through your fear and doubt,
You've listened to the dragon's lies
And trickery won out.
Here is the sword you need
To take the power that he took,
But confusion filled our hearts and minds,
For the old one held a book.

The dragon is a roaring beast
That hasn't any teeth,
And the words within this leather book
Are swords within a sheath.
Take the word of Elyan;
Slay your dragon now,
Know the truth and He will make you free.

"Through the Wall!"

"He that lays down the sea is strong
and knows what lies in deep
He brings all it's creatures to serve his kin neath
waves that never sleep.
His way is safe beyond the rock, though
hidden in the shroud
And he that seeks with purest heart is safe
beyond the cloud
I speak to stone and foaming sea and bid it to be friend
The free bird will escape the snare and jaws
that seek to rend."
Break loose and carry those you love to rest
on peaceful sand
Break free, break through for aid this hour
comes only from your hand"

"Celeisa to Sophia"

"Listen oh Daughter
for wind, wave and stone
have whispered your name
In the voices of water
The crackle of flame
That rides on the breeze
Say "never have you been alone"

He sounds in the deep
And he leads with his song
To a way that is sure
Though the travel is steep
To a water so pure
It refreshes the soul
And the heart will surely beat strong."

"When We Left the Land"

"A sea of tears has come between
The bravest of those that choose
To give their place for love of kin
And great the treasure they would lose
To not see home or child again
To see us safe away

There is no comfort to the son
Or healing of the mother's heart
But proud are they that know a name
Of one that stayed for their own part
We sing now praise and keep their flame
In gratefulness this day."

"Prophecy: The Coming of War"

"When through the mountains and the water
Comes the blood of son and daughter
And new will come among the old
The days of warriors will unfold
The Sandosu will run with red
And every heart will fill with dread
As on its soil the dragon stands
Come through the door from other land.

There is no comfort for the young
Till ancient word through ancient tongue
Has lit the skies again with fire
Where demons hide and do conspire."

"Taliik's Muse"

"The wall will crumble, and then give way as darkness fills
the sky
The enemies will flee in fear when dragon voices cry
And all will fall and none shall rise above the dust of war
For in his tongue comes certain death and they shall be no
more!"

"Sandosu"

"The sword of the dragon will come one day
To the land of the Cintani bird.
When the mountain passes shall fall away.
The trumpet will sound and the shout will be heard
From the hoard that will rise against all that we love
And the earth will shake and the great towers sway.
Sandosu begins at last.

The sun will be hidden and day will be dusk
Till the battle has ceased and the rumblings have stilled
The wheat will remain on the ground in the husk
And the plowman will flee from the fields they have tilled
Then women will hide in the eyes of the mountain
But brave men stand against chance to be killed
Till Sandosu will end at last.

Their hatred is strong and through time and again
They have waited and searched for the door
The oath that has held them is stronger than men
It is cruel and has roots in the darkest of moor
And from somewhere beyond where their memories begin
It drives them to madness and thirsting for war
Sandosu has come at last.

Now come the sons and daughters through ages
With the words that bring us to light
They take to the fray where the dragon then rages
And curses are spoken and he will take flight
Then his screams will strike fear in the souls of the dead
As the truth pierces deep and his teeth cannot bite
Sandosu will end at last.

So cry for the lost and give mercy to those
Deception has buried so deep
They walk in chains of the master they chose
They are bound to destruction in vows they must keep
To a master so cruel and his passions so fierce
But the truth he denies is the pain that he knows
Sandosu will end at last."

"The Darkened Eyes"

The darkest came within to blind
the eye from ancient truth
For lies are deep and fury rages in the mind of youth
Though pain and terror now controls the
hand of brethren lost
And justice cry would be revenge when
valley plain is crossed

There is but one salvation for the children gone so far
When violently they shake His soul and
see of which they are
To one the revelation comes, to one the end of all
When all is lost then all is found at breaking of the wall.

They seek the words that would exalt
and grant to evil heart
The highest power for foulest deeds to rend all hope apart
But it must be that right give way,
redemption yearns to come
The heart that fails will sing again where
all good things come from.

"Brethren Lost"

"Where unforgiving heart remain
The fellowship is missed
And what was one alas is twain
No more they offer hand of kin
But blow to brow that once was kissed
And battle as the worst of men."

"This is not Elyan's way for them
It grieves his very heart
The flame of brotherhood is dim
Dread evil toward the light is sent
But through the book and for his part
He changes all when days are spent."

"Elyan's Shield"

"The shaft is nock and at the call
Of trumpet sent, yet will not fall
For feathers sewn are of the wing
Of foreign bird that cannot sing
Their song of death within this land
Or bring their harm by bow in hand
So fly them all away to height
They cannot sing against the light

The arrows rise but turn their rain
Upon the wolf, upon the Bain
The terror of the sky is not,
Confusion in its stead is wrought
A thunder rolls then splits the sky,
Before the soul can blink an eye
And in its tempest blows away
The song of death sent from the grey."

"The Choosing"

"For love of fair one he will give
The words of life to death, to live
Against all hope we see it lain
For truth is scarce and trust is slain.

The heart is torn to do the right
For good of all or save the slight
But this we deem act of a fool
Will not give evil right to rule

The sacrifice is not the end
His truth of truth does not depend
On mortal men to see it through
The greater love we see him do."

"For what is more to slay and end
The life of one that once was friend?
Or heal the wound and bind the heart
I choose forgiveness for my part."

"The Last From the Book"

"The Fathers fall before the hoard
And dragon reaches for reward
The sun now strikes the broken sword
And all will feel the blow

The earth doth shake as fire falls
And blazes round the one who calls
And from the ancient palace halls
The power now must flow

Oh bring the vision full of sight
Within the brilliance of its light
That strips away the will to fight
And courage flees away

The spoken word from ages past
With untamed power fully cast
On this consuming lust at last
Pours out upon this day"

"Balin's Farewell"

"Journey far my friend
And take for your cloak
Garments warmed in
Elyan's fire
They will keep you from
Weary rains that soak
And will shed all
Evil's dark mire

You will find your way
To a harbor sure
You will find your voice
In his word
Healing comes from you
With a heart so pure
Like the song of
Cintani bird."

ABOUT THE AUTHOR

Jim Cash wrote and sang his first song at 15
and has been sharing them with the world since 1973.
In this, his first book, it was a natural progression
for him to take his ballad style of songwriting
to the next level by weaving it into a book about
a book of songs and poems.
As the story developed, the two elements
seamed to feed each other and he found that
the poetry shaped the very direction of the storyline.
These are his day dreamings and gift to his children and
the all who love to imagine.

Look for the sequel, "Balin's Road".
He has also written several books for young children.

"How About a Story?"
"Jack the Opossum Goes Walking at Night!"
"I'd Like some New Shoes in the Size Number Ten!"

Please write a review on Amazon!

Made in the USA
Columbia, SC
18 September 2017